SIN EATER

Sienna PRATT

Cover : Sos.Samantha
Illustration: Nicolas Jamonneau
Royalty-free images : Canva Pro
Proofreading and corrections : Donna Marie West
Publisher: Over Dark

ISBN : 978-2-494309-19-7
Legal deposit: November 2022

I'm starting this journal today so that my successor can benefit from my experience. So that he too can understand that he isn't alone. And that, despite the fears of self-righteous people, our actions are just and beneficial. If you're reading me today, it's because you've taken up the torch and are now carrying our heavy cross.

Whether you like it or not.

Eltz

1

Believ

I follow in the wake of a man whose footsteps clatter on the gravel. The atmosphere is clammy and heavy, not helped by the fog that surrounds us. Only the sharply angled roof manages to cut through the suffocating clouds, revealing the age of the building almost entirely covered in bright red Virginia creeper. Despite the mansion's breathtaking appearance, an oppressive, inquisitive, and suspicious feeling pervades.

"It's this way," says the man without so much as a glance, as he had stared at me unabashedly when I entered his property.

Although he does his best to conceal it, his unease is palpable. His gloved hand trembles as he points to a narrow staircase that presumably leads to the basement. He's terrified.

How can you blame him?

Everyone knows that it's forbidden to use a Sin Eater. And the penalty for offenders isn't anecdotal, but pure and simple death.

How could we at this point go back and legitimize such radical penalties?

Just a few decades ago, it was abolished in favor of more proportional, humane, and reversible penalties. Why is the simple act of seeking the repose of departed souls such an unforgivable sin that those who do so must be deprived of their most cherished possession?

No matter! Both he and I are risking our lives in this hazardous undertaking, which even the hostile climate seems to seek to discourage. And yet, both of us are determined.

I give him a vague nod that he doesn't even perceive, so tense is he in his collar, his gaze fixed on a redeeming horizon, before slipping down the stairs, making sure to leave the door ajar.

I've barely descended a few steps when a terrible musty smell catches in my throat, accompanied by unfamiliar ferrous odor. Has the body begun to decompose? How could this be? I moved as soon as the news of his death reached me!

Given the magical channels used to contact me, I deduce that the deceased was a particularly important person, or at least one with sufficiently extensive connections for my Brotherhood's hierarchy to dispatch me as a matter of urgency.

It's not unusual for Sin Eaters to be mobilized by dreams. What is unusual, however, is for the request to be accompanied by such eagerness. In any case, last night's dream led me straight here. It's a good thing I was only a few hours away, and that my motorcycle posts the speed limits!

I slip and catch myself *in extremis* on a prominent stone in the wall. I could have grabbed the rope rail, but the protocol is clear: I mustn't touch anything, leave no trace of my passage. I don't know why; that's just the way it is. And ever since I took up the profession, I've endeavored to adhere strictly to the rules, even if I have my doubts about their effectiveness.

The faint glow that filtered in from outside is now a distant memory, and I'm so immersed in darkness that I can barely see my feet. I redouble my caution, refusing to sprawl downstairs because I've missed a step or slipped on one.

Groping my way along, step after step, I realize how uneven, worn, and smooth they are, a testimony to centuries of intensive use that suddenly arouses my curiosity. Who could have gone down there? What were these isolated places hiding? Was there food storage or a crypt? Or, worse still, was it once the headquarters of a sect?

I'm rambling, which obviously won't help me.

I approach the bottom of the stairs with relief, betrayed by the faint glow of dancing torches. You have to admit, they've got theatricality down pat! Did the owners ever think of installing electricity? The terracotta floor oozes, as do the damp walls that reflect the flickering flames.

The body is there, laid out in the center of the room, barely concealed by an immaculate sheet upon which shadows dance. Why on earth do these torches give the impression of being in a draft, when this room has no openings except the one I used to come downstairs?

Although impatient to get it over with, I linger a few moments to stare at him. He's a young-looking man, despite the mask he wears, frozen in eternity. His features are harmonious, and it would be no exaggeration to describe him as ravishing. I feel no more injustice in working with someone who has been struck down in the prime of life than with an octogenarian. Rather, it's the idea of officiating over the dead that still makes me uneasy, especially as I don't believe a word of this Bible that never leaves my side. But I promised. And by force of circumstance and without really having chosen it, I swore an oath to the Brotherhood. I must honor my word, and the only way to do so is to follow protocol and respect every detail, no matter how repugnant.

I reach into my rucksack and pull out the pouch belonging to Eltz, my predecessor. I open the ebony box it contains and arrange the components with almost surgical precision, right next to the body. There's no need to refer to the manual; I'm used to doing this by now.

I place the bread on the torso of the deceased man, just above the small leather purse intended to remunerate my intervention, and sprinkle it with a pinch of salt. I remove Eltz's notebook from the box, place it on the floor, and open it to the page marked by a modest wooden crucifix. According to eyewitness accounts, each of these crosses used by my colleagues contains an authentic fragment of Christ's cross, giving them a divine aura that ensures the effectiveness of our task.

I place it delicately on the dead man's forehead, once again covered in his shimmering shroud, and begin my incantation in a timid whisper that nevertheless ricochets between the stone walls.

“Stop...”

A strange lament spreads through the empty room. I freeze for a moment, glancing around. I can't make out anything but those damn torches, whose wild flickering is seriously beginning to tire me.

I resume in a slightly louder voice.

“Please... stop...”

Again? Have I gone mad? Leading this strange life of mine, it wouldn't be surprising. Without paying any further attention, I concentrate once again on my prayer, which I intone in a more pronounced manner, determined to get to the end of it as quickly as possible.

"Leave me my sins..."

Could it be a sick joke? An idle kid who, if not intimidated by my status, is mocking me and the poor soul I've come to save? By what miracle?

"I summon you to show yourself!" I articulate, unsure of myself. "It's risky to interrupt a Sin Eater, you know!"

"I need to know..."

"What do you want to know?" I ask, still unable to identify the source of the voice.

"What happened to me," the voice whispers to me, now more tangible and hoarse, though still bodiless.

"What do you mean?"

You're out of your mind, girl. As if it's possible to talk to a dead person!

"Believe me, it's me talking to you," the entity indicates, as if reading my questions in my thoughts without my having to formulate them.

That's all I need. It's bad enough that my life is a never-ending mess, but if someone interferes in it, I'm not done yet!

"Are you saying that this body, lying here in front of me," I begin, pointing to the inert remains, "is yours?"

"Absolutely!" confirms the ghost, materializing in a vaporous form above the body.

My work doesn't fit into the "normal" category. It calls on ancestral knowledge and ceremony derived from supernatural practices. After my initiation, my most deeply-rooted beliefs collapsed, and the boundary between what is real and what isn't became blurred to the point of virtually disappearing, even if I sometimes persist in wondering about possible technological remedies that would explain the inconceivable. Who am I to deny what my ears hear and my eyes believe they can discern? I don't pretend to know everything about the afterlife, so I might as well find out more about this apparition, which seems strangely relevant to me.

"But why wouldn't you want me to rid you of your sins? It makes no sense. My only ambition is to offer you eternal rest!"

"What would I do with eternal rest, when I don't know what happened to me?"

Why does this dead man insist on remaining, when he could be enjoying infinite serenity?

"Is it that important?"

"Please," he begs even more earnestly. "It's my soul at stake. Shouldn't I be the sole decision-maker?"

"Some have haunted the living," I retort. "I can't take the chance that you'll show up somewhere. I'll be blamed."

"I promise to remain invisible. Give me the opportunity to understand. I can't fade away without it."

I think, trying to refuse him. He's putting me in an unprecedented position. Under no circumstances am I to deviate from my ritual. The instructions are formal on this point. But what he requires of me is a transgression whose consequences could prove catastrophic for all the souls I'm supposed to save. And yet, how can I blame him? I would have made the same request in his place... if I had materialized after my death, of course.

What should I do? Stay here and force a soul to rest in peace, even though it has no desire to do so, or settle this matter as quickly as possible so that I can continue my work in accordance with the prescriptions of the Brotherhood? I'm aware of the consequences for both of us. Neither of these alternatives offers me a suitable way out. I'm stuck, but anything would be preferable to staying in this nauseating crypt for another hour!

I let out a sigh that betrays his victory, knowing full well that I'm about to make a terrible mistake.

"Will you be discreet?"

"I promise."

"No chains, no night-time howling?"

He stifles a laugh, which makes me frown. A wispy cloud with a sense of humor. I would never have bet on it. It would almost lighten this mission, which seems rather hopeless now.

"Neither, I give you my word. Is that really what ghosts do?"

Excellent question! This is the first time I've come across one, despite my significant experience as a Sin Eater. In fact, I was skeptical until today. I guess folklore is more ingrained in my mind than I thought.

"No idea."

I grab the small leather purse and slip its contents into a pocket of my bag. I'm not very comfortable with the idea of taking these six coins that I don't deserve, but abandoning them on the spot would be tantamount to admitting that I haven't done my job as well as I should have. Not only would I be severely punished, but the spirit would be immediately neutralized; no one would have gained anything from this risky venture.

I put my artifacts back in Eltz's bag and rush up the stairs, determined to get away before I change my mind—as if running away from this unlikely scene would make it any less real.

Before heading off into the darkness, however, I have one final word of caution.

"Behave yourself, understand?"

Nearly four weeks ago, three of my children—Amy, Hugo, and Jack—died. All swept away by the terrible epidemic that has struck our state. They suffered a thousand deaths, slowly bleeding to death, their organs inexorably liquefying. I watched over them with devotion until the end in the vain hope of alleviating their torments. Only Elsa survived. And me. Now it's just the two of us.

Before it was time for the funeral, old Alma, who lives alone on the outskirts of the village, came to visit me. Our community has always thought of her as a poor, confused woman.

Avant qu'arrive l'heure des funé I thought so too for a long time, I confess. That day, however, despite the insanity of her words, I wanted to believe her. She was talking about a secret society that worked for the peace of souls… and the living. The "Sin Eaters." She claimed that this brotherhood of Welsh origin dated back hundreds of centuries and that, thanks to their perseverance, the cycle of reincarnations went on without a hitch. It also prevented the dead from haunting those who remained.

I've never been much into all these questions of soul survival, religion, sin, hell, and heaven. But coming so close to death made me think about it a little more.

My poor children died far too young and most likely don't have such terrible things to make up for. However, I can't help imagining that perhaps Alma is right and that they risk damnation and perpetual wandering. I have to find a Sin Eater, to protect my children in the afterlife. How do you locate this kind of person? What might they look like? How could I recognize them and request their services? Alma told me she didn't know.

She only told me that when her husband died, her brother-in-law had brought one home—found in a filthy pub—who had officiated for the peace of the survivors. And that it had apparently worked. She wasn't quite sure and didn't offer any proof, but she seemed convinced, nonetheless.

Eltz

2

The Ghost

Who is this arrival? How is it that the few words she uttered awakened me from my torpor and brought me back to a relative existence?

I was wandering in the void, drowned in an anesthetic cocoon. Not unpleasant, but not exactly comfortable either, an incomprehensible form of nothingness where a few snatches of nonsensical conversation reached me.

The fall into that sordid cellar felt like an icy shower, while the fragments of formula disseminated by her pale lips pierced me like sharp blades. What a paradox to feel so much suffering for a bodiless being like me!

I'm looking at a... woman. At least, it looks like one. You can't make out much in this gloomy place. To make matters worse, she's dressed all in black. I can barely make out her shape. Her face, fine and graceful, sports an austere countenance that doesn't sit well with the astonishing hair revealed to me by the flickering candle flames. It wasn't easy to get her to admit my presence, let alone distract her from her work. I imagine it's an important responsibility, since the peace of the living depends on the repose of the dead. There's no doubt that surprise was my ally in convincing her. And amazement too, I imagine.

Now what do I do?

My body is preserved for a while longer, and my sins belong to me until someone realizes that they haven't been taken away. How much time does that leave me? In this form, time seems relative and difficult to quantify, so how do I conquer it? Where do I begin to understand who I am and discover the tragic circumstances of my disappearance?

How can I investigate when I don't know where to start? As for getting answers, I'm not in a position to solicit them, at least not without terrorizing people. But I've given my word; I can't risk harming...

Who is she, anyway?

How is it that a frail, innocent-looking young woman like her belongs to the Sin Eaters? Although I'm not familiar with the term, I'm not totally unfamiliar with it either. I've intercepted her in a state of uncertainty, a sign that someone has taken on the task of guiding her to my bedside. Yet she clearly doesn't fit the profile!

I can't let her go like this. She's the only one who knows of my existence and, if I'm to honor my promise, she's also the only one who can help me. I follow her up the stairs, blowing out the torches that lit up the cellar on the way.

Once I've reached the threshold, I step through the door she's just closed and set off after her, despite the pouring rain. She may have tiny legs and vision limited by the precipitation, but she moves fast. Without a backward glance, she makes her way back to the wrought-iron gate that opens in her path. It's as if the locals were impatiently awaiting her departure.

She pulls into the plane tree alley and jogs toward the road, before stopping in front of a sleek black motorcycle. I would have rather imagined her piloting a pastel yogurt tub, not a racing machine, although her dark leather outfit and hulking backpack should have tipped me off.

She dons a matching matte-black helmet, contrasting with her moonlight hair from which only the now-dripping loose braid protrudes, and starts off with a bang.

I mustn't let her out of my sight!

Without really knowing how, I attach myself to her, forging a kind of psychic bond between us, fleshed out by the promise I've made to her. Whatever happens, our fates are now linked.

Wherever she goes, I go.

Despite the torrential downpours, she moves like the wind. Fearless. Unaware, above all! Is she trying to break her bones?

Suddenly, she slows down and turns onto a muddy path leading to a dilapidated barn. What a brilliant idea! Once the bulk of the downpour has passed, we'll be able to resume our journey in more favorable conditions. And be less suicidal about it.

She shelters her machine under the tin roof and sits down on a bale of hay, unpacking the inside of her miraculously still-dry bag. With obvious respect, she opens the black box adorned with a mother-of-pearl skull and reveals its contents: a loaf of bread, a split wooden bowl, a can of cheap beer, a dented flask, an old leather notebook with a small wooden crucifix, a battered telephone, and the leather purse from the cellar.

I'm by no means a specialist in Sin Eaters, of whom I was previously unaware, but I doubt these utensils are the ones traditionally used, if this institution is as old as it seems. Anyway, as long as it works, esthetics are of limited interest.

She grabs the loaf and is about to bite into it. But what's she doing? Has she already forgotten our meeting? And the words we exchanged?

"You've got a short memory!" I exclaim, incensed at her betrayal.

"I beg your pardon? Show yourself, I can't stand talking to a wall," she orders me in a tone that brooks no contradiction.

I don't know how, but I materialize in front of her. She stares at me, dumbfounded, as if she hoped she had just dreamed me up.

"Why are you eating that bread?" I repeat dryly.

"It's probably escaped your notice that, unlike you, I have to comply with my body's physiological constraints if I hope to live a little longer. Eating is one of them."

"Because you're concerned about staying alive? The way you drive, I doubt it. As for that bread, it belongs to me, and I can't remind you enough of your oath."

"My oath?"

"To leave me my sins. Have you already forgotten?"

"Come on, relax! How do you expect me to absorb your sins when there are dozens of kilometers between your body and mine?"

Is that how it works?

"You mean this meal won't have any effect on me?"

"None. On me, on the other hand..."

She doesn't have time to finish her sentence before her stomach makes a loud protest. Indeed, her hunger isn't feigned.

"Forgive me, but I'm just discovering all of this. And as you can imagine, it's quite disturbing."

"Logical. You'd have to be a little bit touched to find the situation normal."

I stare at her, bewildered. Is she *touched*?

"Don't look at me like that. What I mean is, if the existence of Sin Eaters has remained relatively confidential over the centuries, there must be a reason. I take it that most people can't handle such information."

She has a point there.

"The ghost story, while more widespread, is no more widely accepted. These are tales for children. Well, most of the time. And for Sin Eaters, obviously..."

I can see that something is troubling her.

"You've never met one before, have you?"

She nods feverishly.

"Did you believe it?"

This time, she shakes her head. No, she didn't believe it, despite her involvement in a secret brotherhood dedicated to ensuring the repose of the dead. I don't get it.

"Please explain."

"Let's just say that my vocation fell into my lap. I didn't choose to become a Sin Eater; I just did."

What do you mean, you "just did"?

"And you, did you believe in ghosts before you became one yourself?"

Excellent question!

"I don't know. I have no memory of who I was before."

Saying this out loud makes my chest tighten, as if the tingling inside me has suddenly become more tangible. This is my real problem: I don't know who I am. As for my death, it too remains a mystery.

"Don't you remember anything?"

It's my turn to shake my head, in the grip of too much emotion.

"Not even your nearest and dearest, your family?"

Once again, nothingness comes to me. Oblivion has seized every last shred of memory, obliterating my past existence and no doubt the one to come.

"How can this be?" she murmurs, incredulous. "Perhaps your death was so tragic that your mind preferred to conceal it..."

Her guess makes sense. But I like to stick to the facts. And the fact is, I don't know anything about anything—or almost anything—including that which concerns me directly. All I retain are vague recollections that blend different eras and general knowledge.

"Who are you?" I ask, suddenly realizing that I still don't know her first name.

"Believ."

"Mmm, nice."

Although I don't know what I look like at this moment, I try to give her a smile.

"And entirely appropriate," I add, now convinced that our meeting was no accident.

Who better to assist me in my quest than someone called Believ? It's providential.

"Believ, I need you."

"I can't help you. I've got to get back to work," she says, clearly preoccupied.

She pauses, deep in thought, and finishes,

"I used to do all this out of obligation. Now I know it's useful. All the more reason for me to continue my mission, you understand? Besides, I don't really have a choice..."

There's always a choice.

"Helping me will be useful too. Something's not right here. I need to understand what happened, and I can't do it without you to help me investigate. Can you imagine me asking questions?"

"Not really."

"This shouldn't take too long. You do a little research, and I'll get out of your way. Deal?"

"Okay. I give up. I have only one demand: you must obey me without question."

She's my only chance, and I've got to take it.

"You can count on me."

I decided to go to the nearest town, to do some brief research and hope to find one. I spent a whole day pacing the most sordid bars, the least well-frequented alleys. Nothing. No Sin Eater. And no one was able to tell me more. Most were stunned by my explanations. Others, who seemed to know what I was talking about, turned away, disgusted that I should wish to make contact with this scourge. They certainly feared being contaminated. I don't blame them, despite the bitterness that's beginning to consume me. But I can't give up.

Eltz

3

Believ

What possessed you to agree to this stupid deal? For God's sake, Believ, it's not as if you had a choice!

After a terrible night interspersed with nightmares and jolts from the torrential, erratic downpour, I get up, already exhausted and unsure of the decisions I made the night before.

Day is beginning to dawn on the horizon. There's no time for daydreaming; I could be caught.

What's the program? How do you discover the secret identity of a dead person?

The media.

I need to find a discreet hotel with acceptable internet access. In a few minutes, I should be able to find the information I need and get rid of this invasive ectoplasm.

If I'd had a working cell phone—not Eltz's prepaid one, I mean—, I could even have carried out these searches from here, but the precautions customary in the ruthless milieu of Sin Eaters forbid me to possess one. I could be spotted and tracked down, and the consequences of such exposure would be fatal. Better to lose a little time than end up in pieces.

With no news from my stiff, I'm off. Maybe I'll be able to lose him. I check my inventory one last time, buckle my bag, and hop on my bike, heading for the nearest town.

Under the dawn rays, the road is adorned with unreal flashes that are lost in the rising mist. This damned rain has at least had the merit of bringing a little beauty to this dreary landscape.

"It's not this way."

So I didn't dream it. *He's* there.

"Hello to you too," I murmur, teeth clenched in my helmet, without even noticing my unbearable interlocutor.

"The manor house is behind us," he insists.

"I'm not going to the mansion," I retort dryly.

No, but who does he think he is?

"Where then?"

"Into town."

"And my death?"

"That's all I can think about, so don't nag me!" I shout.

He's exasperating, asking thousands of questions that demonstrate his ignorance, while he claims to be telling me how to do things! If he wants my help, he'll have to accept that I work in my own way. No more slavery!

I speed up.

Speed is the only thing that soothes me, the embrace of this air that I'm tearing through and that gives me an astonishing feeling of freedom. I'm not in control of much, and this feeling could fade as quickly as it creeps in, as it probably did for Eltz. Yet it's liberating, almost vital.

Soon the city takes shape, shimmering with the warm rays it seems to revel in. The hustle and bustle of this awakening city rumble along the concrete streets. Workers squeeze into the subway or the traffic jams, while I slip from one lane to the next with the agility of a feline. God bless motorcycles!

Eventually, I find a library whose ancient structure stands in stark contrast to the glass-and-concrete towers that surround it in an impressive wall of honor. Throughout the centuries, knowledge has always had the best places, central and unshakeable in most cases.

I park and enter the monumental hall. My light footsteps echo, ricocheting under the vaulted ceiling adorned with sculptures of plants.

“May I help you?” calls a woman, grimacing, hidden behind an imposing, dark wooden counter.

“I'd like to do some research.”

“The computer room is this way,” she points out with a limp, unenthusiastic gesture.

Her monotone gives her the appearance of a poorly calibrated robot. She's not the kind of person who inspires vocations or arouses curiosity.

I thank her half-heartedly and walk away, planting myself in front of one of the screens already switched on.

What was the name of that place again?

“Is your brain a sieve or something?”

Are you kidding? I wasn't making it up! Not only is he persecuting me, he's reading my mind!

“Forgive me for not knowing a single remote village in Wales! And get out of my head, I didn't invite you!”

“Out of your...?” he wonders with a contrite air before pulling himself together. “I didn't know I was capable of such a thing; you think so hard!”

And it’s my fault too! He's got a lot of nerve, that ghost!

He calms down immediately, which surprises me a little; I had imagined I would have to fight more. I can resume my research in peace, although I’m uncomfortable with the idea that I’m not alone in my head.

One thing at a time, Believ, I think, kicking myself. *Concentrate on your mission. The sooner you find it, the sooner you'll be rid of him.*

And too bad if he heard me.

No matter how much I widen my search, I can't find anything. Apparently, with the exception of the manor's owner, there hasn't been a death in a while. What was the body doing in the basement, then? How is it possible that no one mentioned this disappearance anywhere, not even in a local newspaper? Did the missing person have no relatives to announce his tragic departure?

"What's up?"

"Nothing."

"I can see you're upset; your brow is furrowed..."

Ah, because he also plans to count my wrinkles?

"I don't..."

He pauses, aware that he has once again overstepped the bounds of my intimacy.

"I forbid you to do that!"

"Hush!" a reader tells me from his seat in front of a huge leather-bound book whose yellowed pages creak every time he turns them.

Who do I think I am, talking to an invisible being and tapping away on a keyboard that dates from the beginning of the millennium? A madwoman, for sure.

"That's enough!" I whisper to the ghost. "If you do that again, I'll stab you."

"I'm sorry, I didn't mean to," he apologizes, materializing in front of the computer screen.

It's the first time he's adopted such precise features, far from the vaporous entity hovering over the ceremony that should have rid him of this wandering existence.

His hair forms a perfect wave that conceals part of his clear gaze riveted on mine. His square jaw and slim nose give him a determined appearance despite the doubt in his pupils. He looks so young; what could he have succumbed to?

"We won't find anything conclusive here," I mumble as I stand up.

"Good riddance!" says the bookworm, convinced that it's him I've just spoken to.

I'd love to make that moron eat his precious book!

"At the manor, perhaps?"

"If only it were that simple. The people who requested my intervention have no desire to discuss anything with me. And to tell you the truth, asking them directly questions about yourself would be likely to attract a lot of attention, if not reveal that I haven't done the job they've paid me to do."

He remains silent, as if newly aware of the difficulties that await us if we're to unravel the mysteries surrounding his existence.

What did he think? That we would get drunk playing a life-size game of *Clue*? Having said that, I believed it too, imagining that a few searches on the network would allow me to learn more. That doesn't prove anything, except that I'm dealing with an illustrious stranger who no one was interested in, despite his intriguingly haughty appearance.

A terrible crash resounds in the street, followed by the honking of horns and an anxious hubbub. I rush to the square and freeze in front of a terrible realization: a pickup truck has crossed the road and come to rest right next to my precious motorcycle, mowing it down in the process. Taken care of by passers-by, including a police officer, the driver is conscious. My bike, on the other hand, is suffering from multiple contusions, which suggest the worst.

As if I didn't have enough trouble as it is!

I slip discreetly into the crowd and straighten my mount away from the scene of the drama. Apparently, none of the parts were twisted in the impact.

I cling to the handlebars in despair and ride away, my mind already occupied by the scale of the repairs needed to get my bike back in shape.

A motel. I have to find a motel. The rest can wait.

After a day's research, I realize how difficult it will be to use the services of a Sin Eater. But the urgency is there: my children's bodies are waiting in a cold room; soon they'll be cremated. And there are so many others like them, waiting to be purified before the final journey. Why on earth is it so complicated?

Eltz

4

The Ghost

"How much longer are you going to sulk?"

Believ is silent. It's already been two hours since she uttered a word, apart from a few grunts and insults whose meaning I don't know.

The accident to her motorcycle seems to be affecting her more than it should. It's just a means of transport; there's no need to make a fuss!

When she tried to start it right in the middle of our motel room, where she'd rolled out a translucent tarpaulin, her machine made a strange noise, coughed, then folded up in the same silence as its owner. The impact wasn't just cosmetic, if Believ's determination is anything to go by, as she dismantles every single part she can get her hands on.

"And then what?" I try to keep the one-sided conversation going.

All I get from her is the umpteenth grunt, albeit more eloquent than the previous ones.

With her forearm, she wipes away a drop of sweat that beads on her temple, covering her alabaster skin with sludge. This girl is astonishing.

Who would believe that underneath that fragile, doll-like exterior lies a brilliant mechanic who doubles as an accomplished Sin Eater?

"Hand me the blue key," she orders, pointing to a set of tools spread out on the floor.

"The blue one? Which one is that?"

Could it be that I've forgotten a few basic details, in addition to my own life? Blue is the hue of the sky, of the sea sometimes, but I'm unable to recognize it among the objects in front of me. Could it be that my vision is impaired?

"Forget it. You don't even have a body," she laments, standing up to pick up the object, which for me is just a shade of gray, barely more intense than the others.

I'm suddenly struck by the obvious: I can only see in black and white. As for perspective, I can hardly grasp it; everything my eyes perceive seems to be on the same plane!

There's another detail that annoys me even more: how can I fathom those around me without perceiving their nuances?

"Believ, what color are your eyes?"

"Gray."

Well, at least I'm not missing anything there. Whatever their hue, the sadness in them seems unchanging.

"A problem?" she asks, suddenly concerned.

"I can't make out the colors."

"It's only now that you're realizing it?"

"By what reference could I have noticed, since I have no memory of my past life?"

She frowns.

"Is this common to all ghosts?" she says aloud, more to herself than to me.

"How's the motorcycle?"

She nods.

"I'll have to find a room, but that shouldn't be difficult. Then I'll rest."

After a moment's silence, she adds,

"Tomorrow, we'll return to the outskirts of the manor."

So, she hasn't given up. She's really going to help me. The very thought sends a shiver down my spine. I barely realize she's leaving the room in search of a garage.

Our meeting is providential.

How does she live? How does she support herself? It can't be the meager bursary she receives at each service that provides her with food and lodging, so she has other means at her disposal. A salary from the Brotherhood? Savings? I'll have to ask her, although as far as I'm concerned, it's of little importance.

When she reappears with the lifesaving piece clutched to her chest, she gives me the impression of a child delighted with a stuffed toy she's won at the fun fair. It's as if the relief of knowing her bike is repairable is enough to blur for a moment the pain she feels the rest of the time.

A few strands escape from her unstructured braid as she works to reassemble the jigsaw puzzle that is her contraption and, as a sign of intense concentration, bites her tongue, which protrudes from her fleshy lips. She's a beautiful woman. Of course, I can't make comparisons with others; those I've met so far are just faces without distinct features, and as for those from my past... I'm not in a position to answer.

Strange tattoos snake across her arms, like warnings at the entrance to a protected sanctuary.

With the utmost meticulousness, her slender fingers gradually reconstruct the engine's complex tangle, which eventually returns to its original appearance, minus the grime.

"What are you going to do when we find out who I am?"

She takes her eyes off the bike and stares at me, puzzled.

"Nothing in particular. I'll get back to work."

This unlikely rescue mission is just a parenthesis in her life. But what about me? What happens when I find out? Will I wander alone into the mists of time? Will she free me from my torments? Will she allow me to join her infinite journey?

She lets out a satisfied sigh and slumps onto the bed before devouring the packet of potato chips she's gleaned from the vending machine at the end of the corridor, her empty eyes riveted on the small TV set hanging on the wall. This program doesn't interest her; it occupies her, distracting her attention from what's torturing her existence.

When at last she unplugs herself, she pulls out a small piece of paper from the inside pocket of her jacket, lying carelessly beside her. A worn photo. In it, she's smiling radiantly as she holds up a chubby, laughing child. A memory... How I envy being able to cherish this moment, even if it seems painful.

She murmurs a few words and immediately falls asleep, carried away by a sleep full of nightmares.

I return home, exhausted and desperate. On the stoop, I cry out my helplessness until I'm out of breath, then hide in my living room. Elsa is there, dozing in front of the TV still on. Watching my tender child asleep brings me a little comfort, before I too sink into a sleep heavy with horrible nightmares. The Sin Eaters Brotherhood haunts my dreams. In the world of dreams, I attend integration ceremonies, as well as celebrations for the deceased, without anyone seeming to notice my presence. The gestures are clear, the formulas precise, the effects obvious.

Suddenly, an officiant appears out of nowhere, grabs me by the shoulders and shouts, centimeters from my face, "Join us, Brother Eltz! Your sacrifice will not be in vain!" He then places his palm on the inside of my wrist. White, foul-smelling smoke billows from it. I feel as if I've been branded. I scream and gesticulate in all directions, to the point of being roused from my sleep. Here's the solution: if I can't find a Sin Eater to save my children from eternal damnation, I'll become one, whatever the cost. I have to find out how to do it. In the wee hours of the morning, I make myself a cup of coffee and reach for a notebook and pen—my phone has been dead for a while now, depriving me of the pages of notes I'd become accustomed to recording on it—to summarize my dream. I take care to detail every gesture, every location, every element. I don't know how important these details are, so I try to reproduce exactly what I saw in my dream in the hope that this is the real procedure.

Eltz

5

Believ

From the heights, the manor house scans the comings and goings, an immutable sentinel of this village that would be almost picturesque, if I forgot the reasons for my presence.

Everything seems to be leading us into its depths, when I would rather just poke around. Not only am I not welcome wherever I go, but I don't want to draw attention to our clandestine investigation. I take a leisurely stroll toward the town hall. If I'm lucky, the latest obituaries will be posted along with the ads. Given the size of this community, such an event shouldn't go unnoticed, and neither should a guy like my ghost.

I cross the square under the curious gaze of a handful of pensioners and carefully inspect the displays. Marriages, births, and deaths are well listed in chronological order and according to a strangely contrasting color code. No trace, however, of a recent death, and even less of a victim as young as my deceased.

“Looking for something, miss?”

“I...”

What can I possibly say? *"Yes, of course, my ghostly friend here would like to know who he is and what he died of. Could you enlighten us?"*

Ridiculous!

Especially since, if those who used my services hadn't wanted to hide it, I would be in possession of his identity. Except that nobody has a clue.

"I'm meeting a friend. A rather tall man, dark, with light eyes and a three-day beard. Rather muscular..."

"So, you think I'm muscular?" interrupts the ghost, a sexy smile revealing his perfect teeth, which I forgot to mention.

Did I say that? Did I?

My cheeks flush, as if he had caught me salivating over him. Which is certainly not the case; the guy's dead. D-E-A-D. Well, okay, pretty much dead-turned-ghost, but dead all the same. It must be too long since I've only had to deal with crumbling old fogies—if not already dead—if I'm going to start drooling over the first good-looking guy who comes along. I promised myself it wouldn't happen again; when you consider what the last time was like...

The old man listens, distracted, impervious to my stiff's words, before shrugging and shaking his head.

"There's nobody here who fits that description, or I'd know. You don't often see visitors around here, you know. I'd have noticed. You here on vacation?"

"That's right! In fact, I passed a lovely building on the way here. Do you know who owns it?"

"Are you talking about Sir Jones's mansion?" he asks, pointing to the heights where the property I'm interested in is located.

"I suppose so. Do you know if it's possible to visit it? I'm passionate about architecture. I'd love to have a look around."

"Not that I know of. The previous owner wasn't much of a conversationalist. As for his successor—his nephew, as I understand it—I've only seen him once or twice in the village. Not much of a people person, if you know what I mean."

This isn't the way to achieve my goals.

"It's a pity, but I imagine there are other wonders to discover in the area." I smile as I walk away. "I'll call my friend, who must simply be running late. Thank you for your help, sir!"

"As far as being late, I'm late! I even missed my own ascension," my ghost sneers as I return to my bike.

"Miss!" The old man hobbles after me. "His family has always been loyal to our congregation. If you'd like to meet him, he never misses a service."

I thank him with a nod and step back to think. It's Saturday, so I suppose we'll be able to catch a glimpse of the famous Sir Jones at Mass tomorrow.

In the meantime, we're still in the same place, and just imagining how I would feel in my ghost's place gives me mild anxiety. How can we prepare for the future when no one has the slightest idea what it holds for us, when logic would have us believe that it doesn't exist?

I have to help him. Whether I like it or not, he's a step I've taken as a Sin Eater. Most of the time, it's simple; sometimes, not so much. It's just an obstacle to overcome before I can help the next soul.

"Any suggestions?"

"Not really," he replies, once again adopting a serious air.

"Does this place look familiar?"

"Not this one, nor any other."

Clearly, this damned amnesia of his isn't going to help us.

The only link between this village and him is the manor. Somehow, I'm going to have to find what we're looking for there.

"My body," he murmurs, his eyes suddenly filled with nostalgia. "I can't let them have it."

"You won't be doing much with it, you know..."

"They can still root out my sins and compel me to leave this world, if I believe what you've told me."

He has a point there.

"You've got to get it back," he says, without worrying about demanding more than I can give him.

"You've got to be kidding. How do you expect me to carry around a body?"

"We'll find some way," he continues evasively.

Some way; he's a funny one! Between us, the only one with a tangible body to carry his is me! So, he expects the solution to come from me, whatever it takes. But does he care what I risk if I'm caught stealing the remains of an unregistered stiff? I'm not sure that my clandestine status will have any influence on the penalty, but theft and concealment of human remains, added to the practice of my profession, suggests that I'll end up at the end of a lethal injection.

Stop kidding yourself. You've already been doomed for a while!

I'm used to talking to myself, but I'm not sure I'm alone in my head anymore. In any case, the observation remains the same: I don't belong to those who die of old age in their sleep.

"First, we'll take a look at your body."

"When?"

"Tonight."

In order to become a Sin Eater, I concentrate on my notes and try to gather my memories. It's necessary to be as precise as possible and to obtain the tools that most closely resemble what I think I saw in my dreams. Once again, I wander the alleys of my city, looking for an esoteric store. I've never really understood why anyone would be interested in this kind of thing, even though I've always been convinced of the existence—in one form or another—of magic. Ultimately, perhaps the one we call God is a manifestation of it.

In any case, at the outset, I had no idea where to get the items I needed for my upcoming ceremony. So this kind of business seems appropriate, hoping that the proprietor knows a thing or two about it. And that he's anything but a mediocre charlatan.

Eltz

6

The Ghost

“The way is clear!”

“Are you sure?” she insists, her voice hesitant. “No mutts?”

“No whats?”

“Dogs. Where did you come from?”

Never mind. It's obvious that I don't know a tenth of her vocabulary; we obviously don't come from the same world.

“No dog, I assure you,” I confirm, scanning the gloom.

Suspended on the property's perimeter wall, she takes a deep breath and glides to the other side. She lands lightly on the carpet of leaves that heralds the end of summer and crosses the park toward the sleeping manor house.

The place is silent, with only the cries of a few nocturnal creatures tearing through the serenity of the night. A familiar flutter of wings cleaves the air, then fades as we progress, uncovered, along the moonlit gravel driveway.

Believ on my heels, I take the staircase down to the building's basement, while she struggles to pick the lock. Given the time she's taking, she can't have practiced this often; I would even bet it's her baptism of fire.

Impatient to get back to my body, I sink into the half-light. For once, my condition gives me an advantage!

I slide all the way down. The messy friction of the pin in the lock evaporates into an oppressive, lifeless void. I cross the last step and enter the room, plunged into total darkness. The torches and candles are extinguished, so that I can see absolutely nothing. I'm seized by an agonizing intuition that is confirmed the moment my acolyte joins me, preceded by a diffuse halo.

My body has disappeared.

"It's gone!"

"They were quick," says Believ with disarming calm.

"Quick to what?"

"To move you."

I don't get it. Did I miss an episode?

I stare at her, baffled. Will she finally tell me what this is all about? Why isn't she more surprised that my body isn't back where we left it?

"You didn't think your body would be here *forever,* did you?"

"It was here yesterday!"

"I imagine it's being stored in a cold room while they organize your funeral."

"Cold room? Funeral ?"

"To the morgue, to keep it cool before burying it, burning it, or both."

How can she explain it to me with such detachment? After all, it's my body! And even if the prospect of a Viking celebration has an aura as spectacular as it is flattering, I'm not yet ready to part definitively with the flesh that embodied me so recently.

How is it that I know this people and their customs?

My capricious memory only seems willing to deliver a few isolated flashes and vague knowledge with no apparent link to my existence.

"Don't make that face. We'll find it," she tries to reassure me despite the anxiety that seems to be overtaking her, her hand moving closer to my shoulder before passing through it.

This contact gives me a surprising tingling sensation all over my body. Was she hoping to touch me?

"We're going to have to find out who lived in this mansion," she says thoughtfully. "The fact that your death was kept confidential leads me to believe that someone wanted to conceal it. What disturbs me is that I don't understand why."

I nod. If I had any idea, we wouldn't be here, breaking into strangers' homes in the middle of the night.

"Couldn't we go into the mansion, since we're already here?" I suggest, eager to find out more. "The owner will probably have written down a few things or instructions. You don't deliberately store a body in your own home with no specific intention."

"Are you crazy? I don't want to end up in jail!"

What is she babbling about now?

To my amazement, she clarifies, "You promised to do things my way, remember? I'm not a burglar, and as long as I have a choice, we'll investigate without risking *my* neck."

I understand what's holding her back, but I'm running out of time! I'm dead, and my body has vanished into thin air. If we don't panic a little, I could disappear without knowing what happened to me. I don't want that!

"And then, at the risk of alarming you," she continues, "this unprecedented situation isn't clear-cut: everything points to your body having been removed. I wouldn't want to be next on the hit list."

Would a violent death be enough to explain my condition? There was nothing on my body to suggest that my demise was the result of an unnatural cause, apart from my young age. But why bother to rid me of my sins, if I had been murdered? What murderer would hold a ceremony for the salvation of their victim? It just doesn't make sense.

"Couldn't we just take a look at the outbuildings?" I suggest in as pleasant a tone as possible despite the urgency I feel. I doubt we'll find anything in the stables, but the chapel might give us more information...

Believ lets out a deep sigh that is lost in the breeze. I feel her hair bristle and a slight tremor stir the air. This strange sensation makes me feel her hesitation, her resignation, as if she's fighting with all her might, knowing full well she can't win.

"To return to service, I must first complete my mission with you. The sooner the better. Let's hurry," she insists, imperious.

We leave the courtyard and cross the wooded part of the property, home to a discreet old building. The blackened, ivy-covered stones blend into the ever-present shade. Only the riveted wooden door stands out, illuminated by its arched, luminescent frame. Believ steps over the small steps and pushes open the heavy door, which lets out an eerie creak.

With her flashlight, she scans the room, which reveals nothing of real interest. Exposed stone walls, a few rows of worm-eaten wooden benches laid out on a carpet of crumbled leaves, a modest stone altar and shabby, stained-glass windows through which the vegetation penetrates the sacred precincts. Clearly, no services have been held here for some time. As for concealing a body, the place is too cramped to contemplate it.

"There's nothing here," murmurs the Sin Eater, scrupulously inspecting a small, dried-up stoup.

That's what I see.

Like the cellar from which I emerged, this building is desperately empty.

Dejected, we leave the property without a word, strangled by the terrible feeling that we're regressing instead of progressing, as if instead of dissipating, the mystery surrounding our encounter were becoming opaque to the point of becoming a sticky trap.

We're mired in unbearable ignorance.

Eventually, I found a small, wood-framed shop window with the typical look of an old-fashioned bookshop. All kinds of books and objects were harmoniously stored, inviting the curious passer-by to enter and discover a little more. Encouraged by the diversity of the exhibits, I pushed open the door. A surprisingly smiling young woman greeted me. She wasn't a repulsive witch or a raving lunatic. She was sober and natural. Her dress, as deep green as a dense forest, and her long, flowing blond hair gave her the look of a wingless fairy. Her little snub nose and laughing eyes radiated good humor. I immediately felt serene in her company, even before she opened her mouth to offer me her services. A little surprised to find such a shop, I didn't give much thought as to how I could expose my worries. The idea of revealing my true intentions seemed risky. How did I know this woman had no direct connection with the Church? And even if she didn't, would she have remained so kind to a future Sin Eater? Would she not have turned away from me, fearing for her future? So I decided to remain as neutral as possible and simply list the items I had come to collect:

- a black leather purse
- a crystal flask
- a wooden bowl
- a natural cotton fabric
- a small satchel

I realized that she'd immediately understood my intentions, but she was thoughtful enough not to ask me about my motivations. She simply suggested different models, pointing out the advantages and disadvantages of each. As for the flask, she wisely pointed out that, despite the undeniable quality of its workmanship, it was still too fragile for everyday use. As a replacement, she recommended a more discreet metal flask. Once I'd made my choice, she had me pay and insisted that I beware of appearances. I never really understood what she was trying to say. With what I needed in my hands,

I returned home, relieved if anxious. All I have to do now is learn the formulas and gestures. I hope to be ready to officiate tomorrow.

Eltz

7

Believ

“Why did you say you had to solve my case before coming to the aid of the next deceased?” he asks me, once we've settled into the room of a picturesque B&B we discovered earlier.

“Because that's the rule. I can only help one person at a time. And as long as your death is pending, I can't be called upon to assist anyone else.”

He seems pained to be taking up my time, even though he's in the grip of a troubling condition.

“Why are you doing this?”

“Doing what?”

“Devoting your life to strangers whose fate is already sealed?”

My determination—along with my faith—is already crumbling by the day, and if he adds to it, it's going to get complicated.

“I promised.”

Why is he asking me all these questions? I'm just an intermediary meant to help him; he doesn't care what I feel. However, watching him observe me with such interest, concentrating on my feelings or my answers, looking as if he genuinely wants to get to know me better, I could almost be convinced. But that's forgetting that I've lost the habit of pouring myself out, left to my own devices for too long, diligently practicing a solitary task. Since my encounter with this ghost, it's become less clear. That I've failed in my mission is already unprecedented and revealing, but now I feel the irrepressible need to keep him alive, without being able to understand why. What kind of influence can a dead person have on a living human?

We don't know each other, and he's no more than an ordinary stiff, yet I'm mesmerized by his aura and the presence he exudes. I'm drawn like a butterfly to the light that will fry its wings. But there's no way I'm going to stray from the path laid out by the Brotherhood—they're the only ones who can help me.

"I watched you yesterday," he begins, his voice enchanting. "The child in the photo is special, isn't he?"

Every mother in the world would enthusiastically agree. What exactly does he mean by that? That he's the center of my universe, that's a certainty. As for why I was separated from him, I haven't the slightest idea. And what I'm prepared to sacrifice to get him back? Everything.

I nod, trying as best I can to hold back the tears that crowd the corners of my eyes as they do every time I think of my missing son.

"Forgive me, I didn't mean to upset you," he says sympathetically. "I would have liked to tell you about myself, but I don't know if I even have any descendants. If only I could shorten our collaboration so that you could find him quickly, rest assured I would do so without hesitation."

He doesn't get it. I don't have the strength to explain to him that, like the rest of my existence, nothing is as straightforward as a simple desire. That even when I'm done with him, I'll go on to the next dead person and the next, with no real hope of finding my child, unless the Brotherhood finally unearths some clues and is kind enough to share them with me.

"How did you come by this passion for mechanics?" he asks in an effort to divert my attention from the pain that's consuming me. "It's unusual for a young woman..."

"Why should it be?" I ask, noting that, like any man alive, he seems to believe his peers are more capable than any woman.

"I can't explain it," he admits, surprised by my visceral reaction.

"It shouldn't shock anyone. Mechanics is the thirst for understanding. Pure logic. You don't need family jewels for that."

"Obviously." He smiles.

This simple gesture is enough to relax me. He's irresistible. But who is he? How come he knows so much and so little at the same time?

"Say, without talking about your identity or your life, don't you have a vague idea of your origins?"

"Unfortunately not."

"Because your language is really—"

"My language? What's so special about it?"

"It's downright stuffy!" He sounds like an encyclopedia. Who speaks like that these days?

"At least you're not criticizing me for my lack of vocabulary," he observes, smirking.

"I'm not blaming you."

Despite what I claim, everything about him appeals to me: his aura, his bearing, and his words. Could he be of royal blood? Has he traveled through time? All of the above?

You're going astray!

“Believ?”

“Hmm?”

“Thank you.”

“Don’t mention it. Tomorrow, we'll go to Mass and try to glean some interesting information. Perhaps, in addition to finding this Sir Jones, the priest will say a few words for you.”

“And it's not dangerous?”

“Not that I'm aware of. You know, most of the time, churchmen don't know where the rituals they practice come from. So, to imagine that they're capable of pronouncing a formula that's followed by actual effects leaves me dubious. After all, why would we exist if they knew how to cleanse their followers of their sins?”

“So the Sin Eaters are their shadowy assistants?”

“Well, sort of. If we ignore the fact that they hunt us down like vermin to exterminate us, convinced that our intervention makes us guilty of one of the seven deadly sins: pride.”

“But that's unfair!”

The clarity of his gaze becomes blurred, as if carried away by vaporous whirlwinds. While I've come to resign myself and accept this painful state of affairs, I see that he doesn't. He's allergic to injustice, so much so that I can read his rebellion on his features as if it were a personal matter. A knight in shining armor from beyond, as it were. Something tells me that the horrors recounted in the Gospels should please him.

The time has come. I must take care of my children before they're cremated. I'm not really happy about this way of destroying their poor bodies, already damaged by illness, but considering the price of a cemetery plot, I didn't really have a choice. Especially considering that I'll have to multiply that sum by three for the next forty years. At the very least. Death has already become a regulated, sickening business, skillfully orchestrated by the state and its gangrenous address book. I carefully prepare my belongings, keeping in mind how the "ritual" will unfold. I can't afford to forget anything. Not today. Not for those departed ones so dear to my heart.

The first, and certainly the most important, ceremony of my entire existence. I ordered three loaves of bread from the baker yesterday, ensuring that I had everything I needed. They're a reasonable size, so I can eat all three in a row without choking or risking dropping a few sinful crumbs on the crematorium floor. On the way, I mumble the prayers I heard in my dreams. I hope I've understood them and transcribed them perfectly. Surprisingly, I visualize them without difficulty, as if I'd always heard and said them. I have the strange impression of knowing them intimately.

Eltz

8

The Ghost

Carried along by a horde of worshippers, Believ enters the church and takes a seat in a vacant pew at the back of the building.

The parishioners watch her, suspicious and reproving. It has to be said that her appearance is the exact opposite of theirs: although she has left her leather suit behind and gathered her hair into a firm bun, she remains a dark stain that stands out among the colorful fabrics.

When the priest enters the vault, the congregation rises in a single movement to welcome him in a wave of fervor.

“There he is,” Believ whispers to me, pointing to a short, plump man sitting in the front row.

“Are you sure?”

“Certainly. That’s the man who received me at the manor when I met you.”

“So he's already seen you.”

“That's right.”

She remains silent for a few seconds, absorbed in her reflection.

“So I can't introduce myself to him and ask him questions. That would be suspicious, and he'd immediately suspect something. We'll have to spy on him.”

"Spy on him?"

"Follow and observe him. If he's your killer or had something to do with your body disappearing, he'll eventually give himself away."

"You think so?"

"I hope so."

Disapproving sighs fly around us. Apparently, chatting during the service is frowned upon. However, as I look around the room, I notice that among the devotees are a few uninterested specimens, dozing off or playing with their phones.

Presumably accustomed to intervening on an ad hoc basis, most of the audience punctuate the priest's words with exclamations that resound like thunderclaps under the vaulted ceiling.

Although attentive, Believ tenses up as the ceremony drags on. I don't want to get her into trouble, so despite the boredom, I make sure I remain invisible, imagining the panic my presence might generate. These people are convinced of the existence of their God, yet He doesn't grace them with His presence, unlike me. It's a strange paradox that makes me smile.

Tired of standing next to Believ, I fly over the congregation, then explore the nooks and crannies of the church. To imagine that men were able to build this edifice impresses me, so massive and precisely assembled are the ashlars. As for the organ, I can't imagine the patience it took to build and install it above the entrance.

I slip into one of the pipes, curious to discover what's behind the scenes, and provoke a long whistle that cuts through the building. Surprised by this interruption, silence falls like a blanket over the assembly, who stare at the instrument in amazement, while Believ gives me an annoyed look.

I can't say I've been very discreet in this instance.

After long seconds of silence, and faced with the absence of a culprit, the priest returns to his sermon dedicated entirely to God. Despite the Sin Eater's hopes, not a word is spoken for my eulogy, not even a hint of regret at my tragic demise. Either nobody knows what happened to me, or nobody cares.

When this hypocritical torture finally comes to an end, the church empties. Believ slips through the congregation but is intercepted by the priest, who greets his parishioners one by one.

“Thank you for coming to express your faith with us during your time off, miss,” he graces her, flashing her a smile as he grabs her hand.

How does he know so much? Has the old man already reported our presence? That didn't take long!

Believ gives him a discreet lift of the chin in return, before being approached by our informer.

“You came! Did you enjoy the service?”

“Absolutely! Thank you for your invitation.” She feigns amiability while inwardly, panic overcomes her.

“Sir Jones is still inside,” he tells her, pointing to the building whose foyer is gradually emptying.

Indeed, the manor's owner is waiting impatiently at the altar, while the priest joins him in a hurry.

I leave Believ with her new friend and slip in past her, hoping to overhear their apparently agitated exchange.

“Morgue... complicated...” begins Sir Jones, apparently concerned.

“Not normal... problem!”

“Discreet...”

“Incomprehensible!”

Despite their attempts to whisper, their voices linger on certain words, which come to me in a senseless jumble.

Paralyzed by these revelations, which make me think it's me they're talking about, I'm unable to move closer to grasp any more.

"We've got to find a solution—and fast!" snaps the priest in a ridiculous flourish.

My situation is interfering with their plans, to say the least, but what exactly do they know? Do they imagine for a moment that I'm still alive? That despite having been stripped of my envelope, my spirit resists?

Feverishly, I join Believ, still in the clutches of the old man.

"Your friend didn't come after all," he insists.

"He had an accident on the road," she lies. "So I visit him and tell him about my discoveries to help him pass the time in the hospital."

"I'm sorry to hear that."

"I have to go. I have a visit coming up. Thanks again for your time!"

Without waiting for an answer, she jogs off to her motorcycle and leaves the city center for a less busy alley.

When she stops, I appear in front of her.

"Where were you? The old man almost toasted me!"

Toasted? Like a shriveled marshmallow?

"He was holding me up in front of the church, and I nearly got spotted by Sir Jones! Incidentally, I'd be curious to know what he was talking about with that priest. Not at all clear, that guy. Did you see how he tried to intimidate me?"

"I think he knows where my body is," I say without preamble.

"Did you listen to them?"

"I caught a few snatches. They were upset and mentioned the morgue. Apparently, something was wrong with my body."

"Really? Is that what they said?"

"More or less."

Something is obviously going on.

"In any case, it confirms what we've been assuming: Sir Jones and his manor have a connection with both your body and the Church. And believe me, given the shenanigans the Church is involved in, it can't be anything fun."

By the time I arrive at the crematorium, I'm all set. I stop in front of the heavy glass door opening onto the immense casket display room. How serene it would have been for my tender children to fall asleep forever in one of these! Instead, I'm preparing to cremate them, leaving nothing of them but a fine, impersonal dust. I push open the door. A horde of salesmen crowd around me to offer me the latest wooden box. Overpriced. I decline. "Thank you, but I'm just bringing my children's effects." My answer to these vultures is cold, direct, and perfectly detached. Vaguely disappointed, they turn away and scatter as quickly as they'd gathered.

The hostess in charge of cremation takes over immediately. She approaches in a grotesque presentation, letting her vaporous black dress flutter on her invisible step. A sort of caricatured apparition, suggesting that she might be a supernatural creature, back from the dead. I'm certain, however, that this is not the case. She accompanies me to the morgue, where she asks what looks like a coroner to take out bodies 3,333, 3,334, and 3,335. Numbers. My poor children have become mere numbers, to be archived once the calendar year is over.

Eltz

9

Believ

The first light of dawn wakes me from a sleep that would have been welcome. The last few nights have been not only full of nightmares, but also far too short.

From one discussion to the next, the ghost kept me awake. He didn't have to exert much effort; he's captivating, and I'm particularly receptive. His words glide by, enveloping me in a spellbinding melody. The breadth of his knowledge seems infinite, despite the confusion that persists in clouding his mind. Although he retains no memory of what he experienced, he's able to relate historical facts with amazing accuracy, in such detail that you would swear he had witnessed the events he describes.

So here I am, hanging on his every word, relieved to see him ward off the night and my tortured dreams, before being caught up by my exhausted human condition.

But that's not all.

Between his all-consuming aura and the spacing of my missions, I feel numb, like a spectator of my own existence in a kind of in-between state, the consequences of which I'm unaware. Torn between two addictions. Torn between the ghost I feel closer to with each passing moment and the vocation that keeps me alive.

I stand up to get out of bed and immediately fall back down, overwhelmed by the dizziness that makes the room spin around me.

"What's the matter with you?" the ghost asks pleasantly.

"Vagal malaise," I grumble in a hoarse, sleepy voice, unsure of understanding this weakness that could just as easily be the result of a fatal letting go.

With a little concentration, I manage to get to my feet and swallow a cup of sweet coffee. The sugary taste causes me to grimace in disgust, which doesn't escape the ectoplasm, whose vapors spasm. Is he making fun of me?

"Are you okay? You've never had hypoglycemia?"

No sooner have I finished formulating my sentence than I realize my clumsiness. He's probably been a victim like most people, but like everything else, he's forgotten it.

He frowns before evaporating, sulking. Decidedly, in addition to being touchy, he's a tad proud. And what if he had once been one of those insufferable, unjust kingpins I abhor? Why should I help him?

You're out of your mind, poor thing! If you'd been a saint, I wouldn't say so, but frankly, I don't see what gives you the right to judge him! Especially since it's all just wild speculation!

Okay. If I start lecturing myself, we'll hit rock bottom.

"That's it! Stop your whims; we have to infiltrate the morgue today."

He reappears as he disappeared, a sign that he's never really far away, and gives me a devastating smile that makes me melt in spite of myself.

"Ah, here's some interesting information at last." He chuckles, obviously impatient.

The advantage of being in the middle of nowhere is that the authorities are grouped together in central and adjacent posts. So, I don't have to look very far to find the morgue where my stiff was taken, although I can only speculate, since I couldn't find anyone to confirm it.

After about twenty minutes on my bike, I arrive at the ugly modern building that stands out in an industrial zone on the outskirts of town. While the surrounding area has the picturesque charm of an old-fashioned village, this place gives the impression of a glass-and-steel blockhouse. I deduce that the morgue is in the basement, unless they're planning to steam the bodies.

The first problem: getting into the building undetected will be no easy task. A flock of police officers roam the parking lot, heralding an even greater number inside. As for wandering the corridors in search of the lower floors and the fridge, that's out of the question.

"It's swarming," says my customer, concerned.

"We need a plan."

Obviously, we can't just jump into the lion's den without having a story to tell when we're caught. But which one?

"How about pretending to be a cleaner?"

"Have you looked at me? No one will believe it for a second. Besides, I don't even have an access card!"

"Go to the reception desk," he encourages me pragmatically.

"You're out of your mind, I tell you!"

"Are you all right, miss?" a uniformed stranger interrupts.

Just what we need! An agent strides toward me.

"Yes, I'm new. I'm new. Well, I'm not. I've been sent to replace a colleague."

He stares at me uncomprehendingly.

"'For housecleaning," I explain, before giving him a smile that is as hypocritical as it is radiant.

"Ah!"

He gives me a surprised look, then fixes his eyes on my motorcycle.

"Nice bike! It's the first time they've sent a biker," he raves, clearly interested in my unusual appearance.

While this detail is likely to be my key to success, it will also be my undoing, as he'll remember it.

"I'll accompany you."

Now I'm stuck.

I give the ghost a confused look, which the cop doesn't seem to notice, and follow him inside. He stops at the reception desk and calls out to his colleague.

"Look what I've found," he says. "A replacement for the cleaning. You've got the info for her badge?"

The young cop gives me an embarrassed smile and plunges into watching his screen. His frantic search makes him more and more livid, as if he's blaming himself for not finding the necessary accreditation to let me wander around the building. Poor guy, if he only knew...

"I don't think so," he admits feverishly. "I'm sorry, miss, but I can't let you in without an official document."

His colleague glares at him, urging him to continue, despite his jerky breathing.

"Can I ask you to wait here?" he asks, pointing to the deserted waiting room for civilians.

"Would you like a coffee?" offers the heavyweight, under the saucer-like gaze of the teller, who seems unaccustomed to such attentions.

"I'd love to, but I'd rather have a cup of tea with a splash of milk, if you have it," I say, in a hurry to get rid of him.

He freezes for a moment, unsure whether he can comply with my request, before racing off in the opposite direction.

I sit down on the chair opposite the door to keep an eye on the comings and goings before disappearing.

"Hey!" I murmur in a sort of shouted whisper that makes me realize that calling a stranger without knowing his first name is as impossible as feigning impassivity under pressure. "The ghost!"

"At your service," he replies, striding unobtrusively past the room's glass walls.

"We'll have to be quick. Have you located the morgue?"

He nods, a mischievous gleam in his emerald eyes.

"I'll be right behind you."

Following in the apparition's wake, I run through the corridors. It's still early and, despite what I had guessed, most of the police force must be in the parking lot for the shift change. We quickly slip into the stairwell and make our way to the second basement.

The morgue is there, but it's rendered inaccessible by an electronic door with a sealed lock.

The man carefully opens the refrigerated compartments and takes out the tables on which the bodies of my little ones lie. He's quick to leave the room when I ask him to let me collect myself one last time, before the next day's burning. I position myself behind the bunk beds, facing the door, a way of monitoring comings and goings, while respecting protocol. I place the loaves of bread on each of my children, then sit the bowl, barely filled with a sip of beer, on my beloved Amy's chest. I then chant with rigor and conviction, adapting my words to the one lying before me:

"I give you peace and rest now, my dear child, my sweet Amy. Go no more to the streets or the pastures. Leave the world of the living for good and gain eternity with our Lord. Breathe in infinite serenity and taste the peace of your soul. For all this, I pledge mine. Amen." I gobble up the bread, swallow it with the help of the beer, and place my lips on the tiny neck of my metal flask to blow the recovered sins into it. I start again without delay with Hugo's body. I'm in a hurry, lest the coroner turn up in the middle of a mouthful. At last it's Jack's turn. I've hardly put down the bowl of beer when I hear footsteps echoing in the corridor.

I recite the formula as quickly as I can, taking care not to leave out any words, in case they each have their own significance. I swallow the liquid, throw the still-damp bowl into my bag, and bite eagerly into the loaf. I chew with difficulty as the door handle comes down. I swallow as best I can and blow into the flask, which I promptly conceal in my pocket.

Eltz

10

The Ghost

At the closed door, Believ's features freeze. This was so predictable!

I refuse to be blocked by such a conventional obstacle. Even though this door looks as if it's impassable, I slip into the system designed to collect the access codes or cards and swing erratic impulses. It takes a superhuman effort and, despite my vaporous nature, I feel sweat beading on my forehead. I feel sticky and inefficient; it's only a door, for God's sake!

Suddenly, a click sounds, and the door opens slowly. I've done it!

“Well done!” Believ says with admiration, examining the interior.

She enters the room and slides along a silver wall covered with doors: the fridge. She opens each alcove to check its contents; on the whole, this morgue is rather sparse. With the exception of one old woman who had clearly outlived her usefulness, the cells are empty.

“It can't be! There aren't any other morgues in the area!”

Believ rushes to a sort of disorganized desk, where a succession of sheets of paper are piled in a casual swarm.

"There's nothing here. Just pointless paperwork. If I hadn't seen your body with my own eyes, I'd swear you didn't exist!"

That's a bit rich. If the authorities have no record of me, does that mean I don't exist? That's a bit of a radical conclusion!

"Yes, of course, sir."

A voice reaches us from the corridor. Someone's coming!

Believ slips behind a cupboard destined for the archives just in time. The coroner enters the room, still absorbed in his conversation.

"I understand, sir. It's just that it's unusual and against procedure," he argues unconvincingly. "I wanted to make sure that... Absolutely... That's right. Although I only carried out a cursory examination, given the limited time available, I can confirm that the body was—shall we say—unaffected by death. In short, it didn't decay."

Apparently uncomfortable with having to provide justifications, he balances from one foot to the other at the end of his phone, increasingly preoccupied with his caller's words.

"That's right," he agrees. "That's right. Epidemiological research?" he asks. "I understand, sir. Thank you very much, sir."

He hangs up the phone, puts it down in front of him, and leans against the desk, caught up in his reflection. Believ, only a few meters away, holds her breath for fear of being discovered. When he removes his glasses to rub the bridge of his nose, I seize the opportunity to create a diversion, slip into one of the alcoves of the fridge, and concentrate on banging on the metal door. Against all odds, I manage not to pierce the wall, which shakes under my blows. Surprised by the thunderstorm resounding in his usually silent basement, the preoccupied coroner drops his glasses, which bounce on the floor without breaking. On all fours, he gropes for them, giving Believ time to slip into the corridor.

With her heart beating wildly, she climbs the stairs without looking back and rushes down the corridor. Overcome by emotion, and quite disoriented, she slips into the first bathroom she finds and vomits the contents of her stomach.

She's clearly not used to this kind of operation. While she's usually required to be discreet and curious, she's just thrown herself into the lion's den, only to realize that my body is more than ever lost in the wilderness, and this time we don't know where to look for it.

"Miss?"

The nosy agent!

"I'm here," Believ tells him, her complexion livid, still kneeling in front of the toilet bowl.

While he would have sold his mother to add her to his amateur hunting roster, he now wears a disgusted expression.

"Are you feeling all right?" he asks her in spite of everything, compelled by the duty associated with being a policeman.

What kind of question is that? He can see she's in trouble, can't he?

"I... Yes, perfectly." She smiles at him, one hand pressed against her belly.

What is she playing at?

"I'm pregnant. Morning sickness." She thinks it's useful to point this out to the policeman, who's falling apart even further.

"Ah..."

Well done, partner!

"Could you help me up?"

Forced to do so, he offers her his arm, his gaze evasive, his stomach at the edge of his tense lips.

"I'm going to get some fresh air. It'll do me good," she tells him, back in the corridor.

I'm about to join her when the coroner bursts into the corridor.

"Lock it down!"

"What's going on?" asks the teller, looking up from his screen.

"Someone has broken into the morgue."

"What do you mean? Is something missing?"

"Not that I know of. But someone was there, I'm sure of it. I didn't pay any attention to it when I arrived. I was on the phone with the boss," he says, shaking his cell phone tensely. "It was when I came out that I realized I'd never opened the door!"

"Are you kidding me?"

"No," he replies sternly. I'm not kidding you! The door was already open! And then—"

"It's got to be her!" intervenes the Don Juan, regaining his color, not caring that he's interrupting his colleague. "Follow me!"

I rush outside just in time to see Believ's motorcycle fade into the horizon. That was a close one!

When the coroner enters, I hold my face in my hands, bending over the remains stretched out before me. I don't even need to fake tears; the relief of having completed the rescue of my forever-lost loves sends salty waves rolling down my cheeks. He approaches me and puts his hand on my shoulder as if to comfort me, all the while maintaining a professional distance. In this epidemic context, it can't be all that unusual for this man to see a parent crying for an entire family in his fridge.

With great delicacy, he invites me back to the manager's office, the only one authorized to press the ignition button on the oven. He has to explain to me in greater detail how the next day's events will unfold.

"Convinced that I've given my children paradise, I listen with a distracted ear to a multitude of useless options, which I decline one after the other. Ashes will always be ashes. I might as well not fatten up that monstrous, self-interested little man in the process.

Eltz

11

Believ

I would love to go for a ride on my motorcycle and accelerate to the horizon, but after what's just happened, I'd better keep a low profile on the roads and either walk or take a car. There's no doubt that, even if I'm careful to avoid the cameras, the idiot at the police station will remember my license plate or, at least, the model of my bike, and if I get stopped by a police roadblock, I won't be able to help anyone.

After parking in a discreet corner of a shopping mall parking lot and hitching a ride to my bed & breakfast, I find myself flaked out on my bed, staring at the ceiling as if counting the cracks might trigger a lightning bolt and point the way out of this inextricable situation. But no matter how many times I turn the problem upside down, I'm so mired in trouble that a happy ending seems out of the question. At best, I end up within four walls. At worst...

Better not think about it...

Despite his translucent nature, I can feel the ghost's gaze on me. Is he trying to read my mind, or is he merely scrutinizing me as I scrutinize the ceiling?

How does it work, anyway, these intrusions into my thoughts? Is it spontaneous or does he choose to do so?

Speaking of which...

"What happened at the morgue? I thought you were too unstable to interfere with the matter of this world."

"I projected myself."

Doesn't he want to use even more obscure words, in case I manage to decipher snippets of what he's saying? Seriously, who talks like that?

"What do you mean by that?"

"I had to get you out of there."

"I've never needed anyone. That's not going to change today."

"I was hoping to create a diversion, if you will. It's the only way I've found to intervene without showing my face."

I'm grateful to him for keeping his promise. I can't imagine what state the poor coroner would have been in if he had seen a ghost. I remember parts of his conversation, especially the "epidemiological research" he mentioned. Whoever's trying to hide that body frankly doesn't know what to invent to divert attention.

This doesn't tell me where they might have dropped it, and I'm clearly running out of inspiration.

"Let's get a few things straight," begins my stiff. "My body has vanished into thin air for the second time and left the judicial premises for an unknown destination, most likely a secret one. We also know that the Church is aware of the problems affecting it and that this is detrimental to its plans. If you were a man of the Church, where would you hide a body?"

"Instinctively, I'd say a crypt, but the church we went to yesterday is too central. It would lack discretion, or else all the villagers would have to know about it, which I doubt."

"Everything can be bought, you know..."

Where did that come from?

"It doesn't seem likely. Why bribe a whole village, when you can just isolate yourself a little farther away?"

"The manor?"

"I don't think so. It would be too risky to bring it back precisely where anyone would instinctively go looking for it."

I dig out of my pocket a small tourist map of the surrounding area I had picked up earlier at the town hall and examine the buildings depicted. Some picturesque, rainy villages, castles I lose count of, and a few entertaining ruins.

"And this?" He points, brushing against my hand. "What's this?"

Just as I scan the map and imagine yet another fortress, I realize it is, in fact, an abbey. It's not next door, but on closer inspection, it's totally isolated by the surrounding mountains. In fact, it's situated on a hilltop, which I imagine would help defend the place in the event of an attack; a strategic position that could be just what we're looking for. Who would go snooping among monks who have taken a vow of silence?

"Shall we go?" asks my disembodied sidekick, once again driven by the urgency that has characterized him since we met.

"Now?"

"If we have to get there on foot, we'll need several days. We mustn't dawdle!"

If I have to trudge through the lowlands to get to this perched edifice, it's going to take me a while! And now that the alert has been given by the forces of law and order, hitchhiking and taking the main roads seems risky. We'll have to take the back roads and walk, which will considerably lengthen our journey. Well, I'll have to walk, as my ghost doesn't seem to mind having to levitate.

I gather my things, shrug my rucksack over my shoulders, clip the strap that holds it to my spine, and put my hand on the door handle.

I turn around and stare at the room one last time. There's nothing exceptional about this room, and I have no particular memories of it, yet I have the intuition that as soon as I leave it, my life will be turned upside down with no hope of turning back. I was a respectable Sin Eater; now I'm a fugitive from justice.

In short, everyone's out to get me.

I lock the door and deposit the key in the translucent compartment provided. This system has at least the merit of sparing me the need to justify my hasty departure.

"I'm going to scout around," says the ghost in a low tone. "I'll be back to give you directions. To begin with, leave the village by the road around the river and head out into the countryside."

"And you're giving me orders because...?"

He oscillates between embarrassment and anxiety. He's so expressive that I can read his emotions on his perfect features, as if reading a household appliance manual: clear and unadorned.

"Because I've got to get my body back," he begins in a determined tone that fades as the words leave his mouth.

"Certainly."

"And because I care about you..."

Did he really just say that? We hardly know each other, and in all practicality, I doubt he'll linger by my side once he has untangled the mess of his life and has the opportunity to regain the heavens.

We gaze at each other for a moment, he no doubt more flabbergasted than me at having uttered those few meaningful words so spontaneously. Unless he later turns out to be a Royal Shakespeare Company actor, a contemporary of the author of Romeo and Juliet—who knows?—his gaze isn't hiding anything.

When was the last time a man like that—or any other human being, for that matter—said those unsettling words to me? I'm deliberately hiding my son. It's totally different, and even if it isn't, the memory of his childhood words telling me how much he loved me will eventually fade, no matter how hard I try not to let my memories of him evaporate.

I mentally snort, chastising myself, almost managing to convince myself that these words don't mean much, even though they make me feel so good.

So I don't lift a finger—though my cheeks heat up in spite of myself—and comply. The route he has chosen is precisely the one I had selected. I would rather save time than argue about an itinerary that's not up for discussion.

My ghost evaporates, not without contemplating me in silence for the umpteenth time, as I make my way down the alley. His absence at least allows me to move forward, my thoughts a little clearer. It seems clear to me that his presence by my side, even though I had rejected him completely beforehand and even suffered him to the limit, is becoming normalized, like an extension of myself. I, who know only cold and loneliness, am suddenly embarrassed by an individual I no longer reject with such ardor, accepting him as part of my existence. But living with a ghost is, to say the least, a contradiction in terms.

Before my head gets too full and an unwelcome migraine assails me, I set myself a goal: to finish this day by discovering as much as possible about our destiny.

It's late afternoon, and it won't be long before night grips the village, driving its inhabitants back into their homes. The darkness may be comforting, but it also brings out the fears in me. It was on a night like this that my son disappeared.

One by one, the streetlamps come on. Remnants of those that once held spindly candles, they're now equipped with low-energy bulbs whose glow increases as night spreads between the stone walls.

I hurry through the village to the church square. All is quiet, the doors are closed, and there are no passers-by. I hurry to leave this exposed space as quickly as possible, despite the darkening night.

The alleyway that will lead me out of the village is plunged into darkness; no streetlamps have been installed here. Set below the hill, it's surrounded by two walls that give it the appearance of a tunnel with an inky sky as its ceiling. My soles ricochet off the cobblestones. The horizon is turning pink with streaks of purple, with only the mountains still visible.

The farther I go down this path, the less I see of my surroundings. Only the disturbed sound of the night still reaches me. The breeze rustles the leaves still on the trees, but that's not all. My footsteps aren't the only ones I hear; someone is following me. The rustle of their clothes and the puffs of their breath are so faint that they would easily have gone unnoticed if I weren't paranoid and over-trained.

Ever since Eltz passed his burden on to me, I've been prey: the prey of shadows, the prey of light. My presence is required and, paradoxically, I'm so feared that I'm hunted.

Those who hide in the shadows are legion, and they all want the same thing: to eradicate a member of the Brotherhood. To set God up as the sole savior, while concealing the fact that He has abandoned them on this earth, refraining from offering them unconditional forgiveness. He created human beings in His own image, imperfect and greedy, but expects them to achieve perfection that He Himself is incapable of attaining. What hypocrisy!

Pretending not to have noticed anything, I accelerate to widen the distance between me and this village, where I hope never to set foot again. I follow the twists and turns of this potentially fatal trench, my fingertips brushing the irregularity of the rain-worn wall to guide me.

Suddenly, the footsteps become less discreet, faster and louder, betraying haste. A voice rises in the alleyway and ricochets between the icy stones.

“Wait, miss! Please wait!”

My pursuer's heavy footsteps echo, while strange shadows flicker around me. He's running, flashlight in hand, blowing like an ox, a sign that he hasn't played sports for some time.

I turn around and see the old man planting himself in front of me, handing me his flashlight and, with his hands on his knees, trying not to spit his lungs out on the tips of his shoes.

“Are you... leaving?” he asks me in a jerky voice.

“For a hike.”

“In the middle of the night?” he continues, his breathing still erratic.

“You've never done this? It's an exceptional sensation to walk under the stars,” I reply, pretending not to understand his surprise.

I pause for a moment. *Why did he run after me when he's so weak? What if he's distracting me while we wait for the police?*

"You should try it sometime. I'll leave you to it; my guide is waiting for me."

"Your... Are you a...?" he asks me, without dwelling on appearances.

"A what?"

"A Sin Eater."

How does he know that?

I choke as I try to swallow, stunned that an old man who's probably never been out of his backwater village knows things that are beyond him.

"I don't understand."

"Do you help the dead into heaven?"

"No, I don't. I'm on vacation."

"Please come back for me," he insists, ignoring my response.

While he's still hunched over, his imploring eyes stare at me, as if he fears a curse will fall on him after his death. Has he sinned so much that he absolutely must be helped by one of my own? The Brotherhood will send him someone in any case, so why is he worried?

"I've got to go."

In a hurry to get out of here, I hand him his flashlight, which he grasps limply, and trot away. It's only when the village fades behind me and the night swallows me in its veil of invisibility that I slow my pace.

How did that man unmask me in such a short space of time?

What did he want from me?

And where's my ghost when I need him?!

D-Day arrived. I took my place in the ceremony room at the crematorium. Alone. I didn't want to put Elsa through this ordeal. To be perfectly honest, I really didn't want to burst into tears in front of her. She's already suffering so much, buried under the guilt of her survival. Here, at least, there's no one to bear my overflow of sadness and despair. The relatively large room echoes as the manager makes his way to the control cabinet. I hear a click.

The white cardboard coffins move forward, one after the other, on the conveyor belt that takes them into the oven. Amy, Hugo, then Jack. This short journey takes an infinite amount of time. It seems normal, given that this is the moment when loved ones are usually expected to express themselves and say their farewells.

I'm locked out of time. I see them playing together and squabbling as if it were yesterday. Their too-short lives flash through my mind until they disappear from my sight. That's when the incinerator kicks in. Suddenly, I hear the thud of the torch, the crackling flames, and the moisture leaking from the intense inferno. In just a few moments, it's all over. As simple as that. At the touch of a button, my children's existence is gone forever. They're dust again. I let my sadness overwhelm me and tears flood my cheeks. I'll never see them again, but at least I have the satisfaction of knowing they'll be okay.

That they'll enjoy eternity in peace, waiting for me to join them. That's if, when I leave this world, I can afford the services of a competent Sin Eater.

Eltz

12

The Ghost

If only, like me, Believ could fly! Crossing this hilly region seems to be an ordeal for her, especially as she's lacking sleep and food. Away from the town, there's nothing to pilfer, so she must content herself with finishing the crumbs in her bag.

Constantly on the alert, she struggles to rest for more than a few minutes at a time. Her complexion has become so waxy and the dark circles below her eyes so pronounced that they contrast with her moon-like hair, giving the impression that, of the two of us, she's the one who has passed away.

If anyone should happen to catch a glimpse of her in the glow of their headlights, she would have no trouble passing herself off as a ghastly white lady, minus the dress from another time.

The melodious song of a stream unfurls beneath dancing trees.

"Believ?"

She emits a guttural growl from between her chapped lips.

"A river," I insist. "You'll be able to quench your thirst and maybe even eat."

"Eat?" she asks with a sigh so deep it betrays her desire.

At last, her eyes leave the ground and gaze into mine, a gleam of greed glinting in the depths of her prunes. They're very pretty, even if I don't know what color they really are. Anyway, I give them a light shade, oscillating between glacier blue and sky blue. I could ask about their true hue, but I'm afraid I would look like a clown. It's just a question of cheering her up by finding her something to eat, not of wooing her... Although the idea of combining the two isn't one I'm unhappy about. But Believ isn't a woman of my time for whom dining and being courted is the norm. She lives in a world where the codes between men and women are governed differently, almost at opposite ends of the spectrum.

"Come..."

I guide her toward the lapping water. In the half-light of the night, she stumbles and scratches her cheek on some brambles.

"Fucking useless thorns!"

I stare at her, stunned by this unexpectedly sharp reaction. Since they've succeeded in hurting her, they have their purpose, however unpleasant it may be. Is that so difficult to grasp?

She vigorously rubs her scratched arms, then calms down as she perceives the shimmering moonlight in the crystal-clear water bubbling before us. She dips her cupped hands into the icy current and brings them to her mouth, swallowing long gulps greedily. She runs her palms over her face, diluting the scarlet droplets that have begun to bead.

I gaze at her swollen lips, hypnotized. The innocence of her gestures verges on the indecent, yet I can't tear myself away from the spectacle she's offering me. I begin to wonder about my pre-coma state—since I refuse to accept my death. Did I live in such isolation from female company that I become aroused by it, or is it only this woman who is causing me to feel the excitement of a prepubescent teenager?

I don't know how old I am, but I'm convinced I've had a long life, full of encounters of all kinds. Instinct tells me so, anyway. But I can't say for sure. And now this pint-sized young woman is carrying me away more than she should. I try to pull myself together, to look at her with fresh eyes. Her outfit leaves something to be desired, but I'm responsible for her condition. Her hair, always tied in a loose braid, gives her that unmistakable, fierce air that I like so much.

Her body, which I've had time to take in at length, is fine and loose, all supple... Unconventional ideas have sometimes crossed my mind—what's left of it, at least—imagining her in all kinds of...

That's enough of that! I shake my head. Quite obviously, this kind of reasoning will get me nowhere.

Quenched and clean, she plunges her empty bottle into the current.

"It feels great! The fish, on the other hand, I'll take a pass!"

What does she really mean by, "I'll take a pass"? When? Why doesn't she want to fish now?

"It's freezing. If I go in there, I'll end up freezing to death and starving," she grumbles, taking off her shoes. "Besides, you can't see a thing!"

She's losing me. Why is she doing precisely what she doesn't intend to do?

"Just a moment."

"What's up? Do you have a taser from beyond?"

What's she talking about?

She removes her pants, revealing her spindly yet muscular legs according to the sway of the branches. They're just as I imagined them. Perfect. To my dismay.

When the shadows part, I discover the mysterious tattoos running across her diaphanous skin, right down to the curve of her buttocks, barely concealed by her underwear.

Does she do it on purpose? Just when I decide to think about something other than lust, she baits me? Considering her innocent, unfeigned air, I have to accept that Believ is no teaser, acting as spontaneously as if I were transparent. Which, in a way, I am. Alas, my body, as it currently stands, seems determined to prove otherwise.

Indeed, the tingling that constitutes me becomes more palpable, and I feel the pulsations right down to my extremities. The heat rises in my belly, fanned by this divine vision facing me.

An unforgettable sensation returns to me. Cravings by the hundreds. How can such a phenomenon occur, when my condition should forbid it? However, I'm not dreaming... If I were to lower my gaze to my member, I'm afraid I would discover that it is, despite its vaporous state, in top form. Fortunately, the suit I'm wearing gives me the impression of not being plastered to my body... I spare myself the shame of reacting to the slightest sight of her exposed skin.

“So, do you like looking at hungry chicks?” she asks, dropping her tank top onto the pile of her clothes.

She leaves me speechless. I had thought she was completely virtuous, but I'm afraid I was totally wrong about her. I've been completely fooled! I stifle a laugh, my heart lighter. The lady has a sense of humor and isn’t a white goose. Now I'm on familiar ground. I stare at her with a teasing eye.

There's no resentment in the words she throws at me with a smirk. She's provoking me without the slightest doubt, knowing that I'm harmless because I don't have a solid body. And yet, I dream of pressing my lips against hers and discovering the curves of her body like a promised land that I might tread just once before disappearing. A last wish I'll never get.

"I'm sorry, I didn't mean to make you feel uncomfortable," I say ironically, with a toothy grin.

I lose myself in her silver eyes, caught by her forbidden beauty, before realizing that she's trembling like a leaf.

"Are you all right?"

"It's freezing!" She grimaces, irresistibly, rubbing herself to give herself courage.

"Why did you take off your clothes?"

"I wasn't going to jump into the water with my clothes on!"

"Because you think you can fish better by submerging yourself? You'd scare off any fish despite your undeniable qualities..."

Did I really say those words out loud?

She stares at me, amused, if a little bemused.

"So how should I go about it?"

"With your hands?"

"You're delirious! Who could catch a fish with their bare hands?"

Is it that fanciful? Although I have no memory of it, the impression of having done it before comes to me. And even though I'm intangible, what happened in the morgue was enough to demonstrate my advantage over a mere fish.

"Don't move. I'll take care of it."

"But..."

"That's enough of that! If you turn into an ice cube, who's going to get my body out of the abbey?

She mumbles a few incomprehensible words, a sort of perfunctory protest, without disobeying me. She just stands there, straight as an arrow, staring at me in anticipation of a feat that may never come to pass.

I levitate above the current and quickly locate a school of wriggling gudgeons. These fish are small, but they'll suffice to fill Believ's stomach for the time being. I move closer to the waves, keeping out of sight, and watch the coordinated movements of the little school of fish, obviously looking for food not far from the bank, where the rocks and seaweed are denser.

I'm so close, I'll soon cross the current. I'm concentrating.

One.

I take a deep breath—as if that would make a difference.

Two.

The water continues its course, while the fish gorge themselves on invisible particles before spitting out the sand.

I'm ready.

Three!

Suddenly, as I lunge to grab one of the fish and throw it in the direction of Believ, who seems to be getting impatient, an eel pops out from under a rock and swallows my prey! In my momentum, I grab it instead. It gives me a terrifying jolt I never thought I would feel. Nevertheless, I keep my fingers tightened around my catch and, while tightening my embrace, send it a wave of electricity in turn. It tenses under the impulse, as stiff as a piece of wood, just before I manage to throw it into the greasy grass, where it wriggles for a moment more before coming to rest.

What a creature!

Believ's face decomposes. She was obviously expecting something less repulsive and probably a little less slimy. If she's hungry, she'll have to make do!

"This thing is huge," she manages to articulate, her eyes riveted on the inert eel.

"That'll give you more to eat. Enough to build up your strength before..."

Before what? We don't know what nightmare we're about to get ourselves into, or even if the outcome will be favorable to me. In Believ's words, it stinks.

She has donned her black suit and is now busy lighting a fire, no mean feat in a region as humid as Britain. After positioning rocks in a circle like a miniature Stonehenge, she gathers twigs and a little moss, which crackles under the flame of her lighter. She tries again and again but finally gets it right. A timid fire licks the wood, from which steam escapes. She feeds it for a moment to make sure it won't sputter out, and then sets off in search of materials to make a makeshift skewer. With relative delicacy, she pushes it through the eel's body with a giggle.

"Holy crap! Not only does it weigh a ton, but its skin stings!"

When she puts it over the fire, I see her hands reddened by the stings of the fish, whose skin she should have scraped off before picking it up.

I watch her, powerless and silent. This body covered in light bruises exerts a particular attraction on me and an uncontrollable need to protect her, when in fact it's she who has come to my rescue. How I would love to nurse her back to health, to erase those painful scratches, to hold her close like a treasure, to admire her until my pupils burn, to make her mine and keep her by my side.

All sorts of images flash through my mind. Burning, exciting, even sweet. Then I come back to reality, hers and now mine, albeit incongruously: I'm dead and, in absolute terms, I'm going to stay that way.

Sitting on the grass, she loses herself in the contemplation of her meal, which she turns from time to time. What's on her mind?

After a moment of eternity, she begins to tear away the shreds of flame-blackened skin to reach the white, translucent flesh. She takes small pieces and shyly stuffs them into her mouth.

"It's delicious," she enthuses, biting into the dripping fat.

It certainly is. Like the moment I savor, before returning to the uncertainty of my fate.

It's my turn to forget what's around us and, as I cling to her glossy, luscious lips nibbling away the fat, I find myself hoping, terrified that soon we'll reach the end of this insane journey.

No sooner has she finished her meal than she smothers the fire and stands up.

"What are you doing?" I ask, displeased to be disturbed in my divine observation.

"It's time to go. They won't be long."

"Who's 'they'?"

"No idea. Church henchmen, I suppose. The police... There's no shortage of pursuers these days."

"How would they find us here? Who would look for a fugitive in a place like this?"

"On the contrary, it's exactly the kind of place you'd look for someone trying to hide. We have to go," she insists.

Whatever the reasons... wherever she goes, I go.

This problem keeps going round and round in my head: how can I get hold of a competent Sin Eater? I keep thinking back to the difficulties I encountered a few days earlier in hiring one. Then I imagine the distress of other parents who, unlike me, didn't see the solution. I can't bear to leave them in this pain, beyond the loss of a loved one. Despite my fears, I've managed to get my family into heaven without too much difficulty. I must continue on this path and offer peace to others. More than a duty, I see it as a vocation. So, I've formally decided to leave everything behind to become Sin Eater.

Do I even have a choice? I don't know and probably never will. However, taking this decision in such a categorical way puts my mind at ease. I feel a bit better, more in tune with myself and, above all, in perfect coherence with my convictions. Following this major turning point in my life, the strange dreams have multiplied. Hardly a night goes by without nightmares invading my sleep. Is the secret Brotherhood of Sin Eaters using this method to distill information for me? An intuition one day, a vision another; all lead me to desperate families in search of salvation for someone they've lost.

Eltz

13

Believ

I walk part of the night with only a will-o'-the-wisp ghost to guide me through this darkness I could cut with a knife. Although neither he nor I would admit it, something decisive happened at the river; the barriers erected between us crumbled, dispersing an unsettling unease.

No one's fooled by the inexplicable alchemy that binds us together, which nonetheless hampers our prospects; how can we envisage a future when one of us is dead and the other is sure to die soon?

Scattering the traces of our passage, we move forward, progressing along paths invaded by sharp greenery and through dense undergrowth surrounded by a silence heavy with undertones and impossible expectations.

I can't take it anymore.

Determined to fill this emptiness to avoid my existential questions, I return to the circumstances of our departure, which I still can't explain to myself.

“Something strange happened when we left the village,” I begin. “The old man...”

The ghost freezes and turns toward me. The glow emanating from his body allows me to discern the surprise on his worried features.

"What happened?" he asks immediately.

"He came after me. Don't worry, he didn't hurt me—well, not yet—but he challenged me."

I inhale deeply and tense up before letting go of the essence of this exchange. "He knew."

"Knew what?"

"What I am. He *knew*."

Again, the silence stretches out, a sign that what alarms me is indeed worrying.

"He begged me to come back for him."

"Did he? Did he really fear for the salvation of his soul?"

I shrug vaguely. "What do I know? To be so insistent, he must have a few skeletons in his closet. Who doesn't? Unless... Maybe he's a serial killer who stuffs his victims in his attic."

Don't overdo it; you're getting paranoid!

What really gets me is how he found out about my profession. With the exception of my tattoos, which I'm careful to hide wherever I go, there was nothing he could do to unmask me! So how did he find out?

"Isn't there anything about your appearance that's conducive to finding out?" My deceased interrogates me with timing that leads me to believe that, once again, he has penetrated my mind without my consent.

"No. Nothing, except my hair. It used to oscillate between chocolate and honey. As I worked, it gradually faded until it turned completely white."

"Oh, so that's it..."

Did he really think I was born with snowy hair? I'm not a mummy! Although... My constant state of fatigue might suggest otherwise. Exhausted, I struggle to get going again, following in the wake of the ghost who's gone mute once more; paradoxical king of both silence and eloquence.

"Can we take a break?"

The apparition faces me and gives me a sympathetic smile before pointing to a natural alcove between the roots of a large trunk.

"You rest. I'll keep watch."

I settle down on the opulent moss and curl up to protect myself from the biting cold. Surrounded by roots, I'm protected from the onslaught of the wind. I rest my head on my rucksack, untie my hair, through which the night air rushes, and close my eyelids. Behind my back, I feel the presence of the specter settling beside me.

Although I'm exhausted, sleep is slow in coming. Now that I'm motionless, the cold creeps into my clothes, sending a shiver down my spine.

"Are you all right?"

That husky timbre envelops me in a wave of sweetness. Despite the atypical nature of this situation, I'm no longer alone. Someone is watching over me, at least for a while. And even if I'm apprehensive about the ephemeral nature of this presence by my side, for now it's enough to fill the void that surrounds me.

I turn around abruptly and find myself face to face with the entity, whose ember gaze immediately plunges into mine. The way he stares at me thrills me, as if he's stripping me bare and making me his own.

"Believ," he murmurs, panting, putting his hand on my cheek.

His touch sends another shiver down my spine, making me tremble from head to toe. I palpitate. Did he really just touch me? I place my hand on his. The pulp of my fingers sink delicately into his flesh before falling through it.

I touched him!

"I..."

What could I possibly say to him? Not only am I so overwhelmed by his supernatural magnetism that I can't string three words together, but anything I might say won't change a thing: our relationship is just a sweet illusion that will fade as soon as he has the chance to return to the heavens.

“Here I am.”

His voice mingles with the howling wind. Surprisingly, I'm no longer cold. He runs his fingers through my hair and slowly leans over to place his lips on mine. He closes his eyes and embraces me. I feel his power, his flesh, and his desire. His body, which never existed before, now presses against mine, while his tongue explores my insatiable mouth.

I want him.

However, just as I had feared, he eventually loses the solidity that was just beginning to fill me up and, in his rush, runs right through me. I imagine this demonstration took a lot of energy. I bite my lip as if to rekindle an aftershock of that contact, to remember that tonight, for just a moment, I came back to life.

On his perfect face, I read immense frustration. I imagine it's visible on mine too, even if this brief closeness was enough to put a smile back on my face for the night.

“Say, will you lie down with me?”

I've dared to make this request out loud. I feel dizzy, a soft shiver running down my spine at such audacity—or recklessness. I feel ready to embark on an unknown path. Here I am, having had only fleeting, sporadic affairs in recent years, congratulating myself on leaving them in the early hours of the morning, asking an impalpable being to hold me in his arms. He stares at me without answering, his eloquence evaporating along with his consistency. I'm no longer interested in his words—at least, not tonight. His mere presence is enough to make me feel invincible. Even if I were to perish tomorrow—which isn't at all hypothetical—I know he would be there to welcome me. His warmth won't save me from a fatal destiny, but at least it has the merit of freeing me from my fears.

I take refuge in the hollow between the roots, my eyes still locked on his, my hand outstretched in an invitation to join me. He smiles tenderly and moves closer. Finally, he melts on me, materializing again, as if his desire alone could make him tangible. And Lord! He seems to want me as much as I want him! Once again, his mouth devours mine before leaving me panting.

"I'll stay with you," he whispers, his breath warm against my ear.

This simple phrase makes my whole body vibrate. Beyond the person who uttered it, this promise is just as unreal. And yet, I want to believe in its veracity, like a fundamental, inescapable, and urgent need. To no longer feel alone, to fill a void.

I'm probably crazy for clinging to the possibility, just as I hold onto his shoulders as he lies on top of me, the weight of his body that of a slender yet muscular man. To further convince myself, I palpate his shoulders and arms as his mouth migrates down my neck, dotting it with feverish, ravenous kisses. The bulge I feel against my crotch raises the fever between us. One of his thighs spreads my legs, while he rubs himself languorously against me, caressing my curves with delight, turning my head inside out. What are we going through? I don't want to think about it anymore, I just want to enjoy this moment and, above all, I don't want it to end... Better still, I want us to go even further.

My latest nightmare has made me realize the absolute necessity—if I wish to be reunited with my family when I die—of training a successor. It's an imponderable imperative if I don't want to end up cursed forever. Strictly speaking, it's not a question of transmission, but of passing on. To be Sin Eater is to build a bridge between the dead, to brandish a sword of defense for life. At no point is it a question of carrying the sins of others forever, nor of assuming them when the time comes for us to die. But to get rid of them and enjoy a happy eternity, it's necessary for someone to take up the burden.

This mechanism is a bit of a win-win: I get to go to heaven, while the world discovers a new Sin Eater. The only one to lose out, in short, is the one who is most interested in this new adventure. It's deeply unfair, but that's the way life is. So I'm gathering as much information as possible for my successor, even before I know who he or she will be. I sometimes broach the subject and prospect, mostly when I'm out and about, with people whose zest for life isn't obvious. It's eminently complex, but I secretly hope that the opportunity to help others will cheer them up. Naturally, every one of them turns away from me when they realize who I am and what I do.

I'm not surprised, even if I deeply hope to find the one who will take up my cross in advance. After all, no one dreams of damning themselves for others. Altruism is out of fashion in this world of indifference.

Eltz

14

The Ghost

Believ finally falls asleep and, unlike previous nights, her angelic face is serene. Her moon curls encircle her pale cheeks, giving her features the appearance of a celestial divinity. I lose myself in the contemplation of this perfection destined for a tragic end, powerless and unhappy. Yet a part of me, hitherto unknown and probably always demented, yearns for her, the sensation of unfinished business nagging at me. I can't think of anything else right now, when she's putting her life on the line to save mine. Or what's left of it.

What benefit could there be in this unnatural attachment? She alive, I dead... How can we ever hope to be reunited? The fact that death might bring us together isn't a cause for rejoicing; it's her liveliness and mysterious curves that I want to enjoy.

Our fleeting contact was exhilarating, but when it broke, it shattered me in the process. As soon as it happened, it was already part of my past, an exclusive memory that I still have. I don't know if I would have preferred to do without it. From now on, I'll regret that it was so short and that it can never happen again. Because even though I'm dying to repeat the experience, the energy these kisses have cost me is far too great.

I force myself to consider this evolution in our relationship with a cool head, before I lose it completely. In concrete terms, I can't risk jeopardizing my future to satisfy this primitive attraction, however tasty it may be. This realization gives me the ephemeral impression of at least having control over one part of my existence, since I've been deprived of the possibility of governing the whole of it.

And what's next on this journey?

Despite our innumerable detours and appalling slowness, it won't be long before we reach the abbey and, if we're not mistaken, get our hands on my remains.

What next?

What will I do with a body I can't occupy? How can I find out what they insist on hiding from me? Assuming success, what will become of Believ? Will she continue on her way, as if I had just been an accident on her way, or will the revelation of my identity turn everything, including her life, upside down? I can't help imagining her in my future. If I've concealed my past, there's little chance of the same happening to my present. I was a blank page that quickly filled up with her.

Deprived of memories, I struggle to understand what interest anyone could have in concealing my death, unless I was once an adored leader and my loss elevates me to martyrdom. That would be flattering but astonishing. And in such a case, I fail to see how my disappearance could have gone so unnoticed. What I don't understand are the motives and the stakes involved in this whole affair. Nothing seems to add up, and the few elements we have at our disposal don't seem to corroborate any of our speculations. We're plunged into a constant vagueness, the opacity of which I find insoluble.

Believ's serenity suddenly seems to fade, and she becomes agitated in her dreams, putting a tortured expression on her writhing face. Twitching, she trembles. Could it be her child haunting her dreams?

A creak breaks the silence of the night. Someone is coming. We've got to get out of here.

"Believ!" I call out in a shouted whisper, while miming a punch on her shoulder. "Wake up!"

She straightens suddenly, like a puppet on springs, and furrows her brows, obviously concentrating on listening to the movements around her.

Another twig snaps, even closer than the first.

"Let's go," she tells me, putting her bag on her back with a calmness that gives no hint of the startle of her awakening.

I don't know what kind of training she's had, but in a split second, she blends into the background with the agility and stealth of a lizard. She strides briskly between the branches before leaving the forest canopy and running up the hillside. She's hardly out of breath.

When she finally slows down, she asks me, "Did you see anything?"

"Unfortunately, I couldn't make out anything conclusive in the darkness. It could just as easily have been a deer."

"I doubt it."

She seems unconvinced by my suggestion. However, I can't imagine why anyone would want to go after her. Why would anyone go to such lengths to track her down in the farthest reaches of Wales? Is she that important? And who would be after her? The Church, for whom she's a sinner, or the Brotherhood, which she deserted just a few days ago to come to my rescue?

We make great strides over the uneven ground, sinking knee deep into the tall grass. Pushing the limits of her endurance, Believ keeps up the pace until the sun floods the valley, revealing before us the abbey overlooking us from its peak.

"Finally..." Believ says with a sigh before collapsing in a flower bed at the entrance to the village.

Although she's awake, her body is spasming again. I go over and kneel beside her, but I'm unable to touch her or bring her to. She's in a kind of trance that shakes her with rare violence.

Could she be suffering from a pathology that explains these recurring symptoms?

When at last her body lies still and relaxes, and her eyes regain a semblance of lucidity, she stares at me resignedly.

"What just happened?" I ask her, upset at seeing her suffer without being able to help.

"I don't know. Probably a hypoglycemic attack."

Despite what she claims, the way she's tightened her lips as if to prevent them from saying anything more shows that she's not unaware of what's just happened to her. Why won't she tell me? What is she afraid of me for? She may be ill, but I'm dead!

After a few minutes and several long swigs of water, she pulls herself together and sets off across the village, her gaze fixed on the mist-shrouded abbey. The magnificence of this edifice makes it unthinkable that atrocities could take place here. And yet...

Bypassing the village center, Believ weaves her way through the barely awakening alleyways back to the small mountain where our destination is perched. She wolfs down a scone from a modest bakery and begins our final ascent. That is to say, before the one that will take me to heaven, as she promised.

Discretion is more important than ever, but Believ takes the main route, which is already steep. Climbing up the hillside would be pointless; with no trees, we're inevitably exposed to the sight of the monks above us.

Having remained silent until now, I can't help questioning her.

"What's the plan?"

She turns to me with a raised eyebrow, then gives me an almost candid half-smile.

When her face lights up like that, I could say to her, "Let's leave; let's leave this place. Let's live somewhere else." What's going through my head to want this cumbersome body that obviously doesn't want me back? But I don't. The force pushing me toward my carnal envelope seems even more powerful than the feelings I'm developing toward this woman. And that's a blow to my morale. Am I as evaporated as my solidity?

"The plan? Get in undetected and snoop around for your body."

As simple as that! How could I not have thought of it myself?! This girl is fearless, no doubt about it. I have no fears about my immediate fate: I'm invisible, except to her, so who could attack me? No one. Believ, on the other hand, is an ideal target. And if I manage to materialize under certain circumstances, there's no guarantee that I'll be able to do so again if she's in danger. There's a gulf between my burgeoning need to protect her and my ability to do so. A feeling of helplessness and uselessness has been building up in my heart for some time now, and it's undermining me deeply.

So, I insist—a bit clumsily, I admit, "Of course, but in concrete terms?"

Her smile fades in the face of my preoccupied expression, and her eyebrows frown delicately. Suddenly serious, she replies,

“I've no idea. I've been trudging through the pampas for three days, trying not to lose my skin. I don't even know what this abbey looks like from the inside, or how many monks there are.”

It's true that our research hasn’t proved fruitful. This congregation jealously guards its secrets and all information concerning it.

“We go in and improvise.”

Just as I said: a real hothead.

How can I be sure that, when the time comes, someone will look after my soul? At the end of this notebook, I've drawn up a step-by-step instruction manual. The essentials are recorded down to the smallest detail. [...]

Practical Guide for Successors

To whoever will devote himself for the salvation of my soul and that of the deceased who will follow me, it's imperative to respect the modalities hereafter exposed:

1. Take possession of my belongings and make sure to find my bag, my purse containing six coins, my sin flask, my stole, and my wooden bowl;

2. Perform the first ceremony on my person, following the usual procedure;

3. Remain discreet to maintain a semblance of social life; the mission must remain secret, as must the Sin Eater's identity.

Eltz

15

Believ

Built like a fortress, the abbey is surrounded by a thick wall whose only visible entrance is a monumental riveted wooden gate protected by a portcullis.

Despite the number of monks I imagine must reside here, the place is quiet. Perhaps a little too quiet. Only birdsong and the whispering of the wind animate the place. Have they taken a vow of silence?

If this building was indeed originally intended to withstand a siege, it must have alternative accesses. I'm not sure what I'm looking for—tunnels, back doors, or some other way of getting back to the village or countryside undetected.

I follow the walls, my fingertips resting on the stone at eye level. The property is so vast that it takes me a little over an hour and a half to complete the circuit without having detected a single entrance.

"Any ideas, Einstein?" I ask, discouraged, as my specter twirls before me, perplexed.

Since our destination is in sight, he seems more preoccupied than usual. How I can sense his feverishness when he's currently in a foggy state, I don't know. But it's impossible to deny that he's stressed. I can understand that his desire to find his body takes precedence over everything else, and that the stakes are high, but we're getting closer to the goal. Why this taciturn look? He should be thrilled. Okay, it's a bit early to be claiming victory, but all the same, a little optimism would go a long way.

"Let me think," he replies after a moment. "The idea being to conceal all comings and goings, I wouldn't imagine that the access is here. In the event of a siege, it would be immediately detected and could be a disadvantage to the attackers."

"So?"

"We're too close. We need to distance ourselves to see the big picture."

"Now you tell me?"

As I was saying, my ghost's "mind" is elsewhere. When you put it like that, it's kind of comical, but it's impossible to describe it any other way.

"I didn't think of it before, I admit," he apologizes, confused.

He avoids my gaze. I'm beginning to wonder if he's a lunatic.

"Which way?"

We're surrounded by hills that all look the same: greasy grass as far as the eye can see, and the odd bushy grove.

He materializes his hand to take hold of mine and pulls me a little lower. One by one, he examines every unusual feature. Every bush, every stone is thoroughly inspected. Yet the morning goes by without us detecting the slightest trace of passage.

Discouraged, I sit down on a rock. At the same time, the rain invites itself into the game. Just what I needed! I'm already freezing, but if I'm soaking wet, I'm going to die before someone else does me in!

"Have a look!"

What's he raving about now?

"The rain, it's pouring."

Fabulous! The rain is pouring. Now, that's a useful observation!

I let out a nervous laugh. He stares at me, a little offended. I should explain to him how weary I am, struggling with physical and human contingencies, which he seems to have totally overlooked. Anyway, I let myself go and enjoy this moment, a veritable beneficial outlet.

"Stop laughing at me and watch a little more carefully," he snarls, following the current as it makes its way downhill before disappearing underground.

My mirth ceases as suddenly as it began. I leap to my feet and approach him.

"A spring?"

"Underground!"

He disappears behind a bush. What the hell is he doing?

Cautiously, I push aside the branches and discover a low stone arch concealed by moss and a large quantity of leaves. As I approach, I realize that it covers a narrow staircase that plunges into the bowels of the hill. I push open the wrought-iron gate and enter the dark passage.

I don't have much to go on; once at the bottom of the stairs, the little light that had penetrated the passage is swallowed up by darkness. Deprived of my sight, I grope feverishly, my head cradled in my neck so as not to scrape the overly low ceiling. Should I move on or turn back before it's too late? If someone comes upon me here, I'll have no way of hiding or escaping.

It's downright risky, especially since, if this passageway exists, there must be others that are more accessible and less oppressive.

I freeze, hesitant. My heart is beating so fast it feels like it has migrated between my eardrums. I take a few steps forward when something brushes against my calf!

Because there are bugs here too?!

Trying to escape, I nearly slip on the damp, uneven cobbles; the perfect combination to end up in pieces.

Where's that damn ghost hiding? Now's the time I need him to glow in the dark!

"Hello?"

My voice, already weak, chokes without finding an echo.

I'm on my own.

For now.

"Roland[1], answer me..." I beg, not knowing whether to scream to get him back or whisper to avoid being spotted.

I'm really going to have to give my sidekick a name, as calling him out without offending him is becoming increasingly complex.

What the hell is he doing?

I should have grabbed the old man's flashlight when I left him because right now, if I get to the end of the tunnel without spraining something or getting mauled by vermin, I deserve a medal.

"Casper? Yoo-hoo!"

I oscillate between terror and exasperation. Why is it that, in critical moments, I always find myself without support? When it came to feeling me up, there were plenty of people around, but now that I need a guide, my stiff is

---

[1] In reference to folklore linked to the ghost of Sir Roland Rhys, accompanied by his pet ape, present at Carew Castle in Pembrokeshire.

nowhere to be seen. Shit, it's for him that I'm throwing myself into the lion's den; he could at least pretend!

"Shhh! We're going to be spotted!" he asserts in a whispered shout that sends me over the edge.

"Where the hell have you been?"

"Scouting. It's this way," he points out, while I'm still drowning in the gloom.

"Light?"

"Ah, yes, forgive me."

And there he goes, phosphorescent again, moving forward into the tunnel, which I discover to be infested with rodents of all kinds. A real pleasure. After a few meters, the discomfort of the situation becomes even more pronounced. Not only am I folded in half, but the track is winding as it climbs. The cobblestones are dotted with hollows and bumps, a veritable obstacle course, which alone demonstrates the motivation of those who once walked it.

I don't know if my ghost is aware of the point to which I'm physically surpassing myself. If not, I'll be happy to remind him. And it's all for nothing!

I grumble inwardly. Yes, well, no one has physically restrained me, let's be honest, him less than anyone. I'm doing all this to... The answer won't pass my lips.

Finally, we come to a grayish wooden door—probably original, given its faded appearance—which seems to lead to a basement. Or more accurately, a crypt.

"What do we do?"

Panic overwhelms me. That my job is creepy as hell, I freely admit, but this is the first time I've broken into private property—okay, the second, if you consider Sir Jones's mansion—and desecrated a religious enclosure. Not that I'm particularly observant or even religious, but it does give me a strange feeling.

“The wisest thing to do would be to wait until nightfall. I imagine that after a certain hour, the corridors are less crowded.”

He has a point there.

“And where do we start?”

Here I am, getting annoyed by his slightly anxious questions, and now I'm imitating him. On the other hand, my ghost never loses patience and answers calmly, without panicking.

“Upstairs. That way, we'll be back down here at the end of the night, and we’ll only have to leave in the early hours of the morning. Hopefully, we'll have found the answers we were looking for in the meantime...”

The memory of my expedition around the abbey comes flooding back. I may have been slowed down by my inspection, but the estate was nonetheless immense. Will a single night be enough to complete the tour?

“I'll have a look around in the meantime, scouting around in case I spot something...”

How convenient to be a ghost!

And what do I do in the meantime?

Will I have to wait several hours in total darkness with only rats for company?

So it seems.

I'd just arrived at the Grand Hotel and settled down at the bar to order the strongest rotgut on the menu, when a young man in his early twenties approached me. After sitting down on my right, he stared at me with his cobalt eyes, a boyish grin lighting up his perfect face. "You're a Sin Eater, aren't you?" he asked, euphoric. At the time, I didn't know what to say, so stunned was I that he'd unmasked me so easily, and that he hadn't turned on his heel, afraid or disgusted to be around someone like me. He must have read my surprise, because he quickly continued, "Don't worry, I'm one too. Christy," he introduced himself, holding out his hand.

I squeezed it nervously. There was a Sin Eater right there in front of me! It wasn't for lack of looking for one for months! But it's precisely when I'd given up hope that Christy presented himself to me! Despite the shock, I instantly felt less alone. So there were others like me. And the one in front of me seemed to lead a perfectly decent life. Nevertheless, I wondered how he'd spotted me. He told me he'd noticed the tattoo on my wrist and the pronounced whiteness of a lock of my hair. Of course, how could I have forgotten these "details"? He told me that he too had felt the burn when it appeared on his forearm, at the very moment when he'd decided to become a Sin

Eater, to save the soul of his sister who had died suddenly, in circumstances that remain enigmatic.

Apparently, the loss of a loved one is the common denominator of all Sin Eaters. That's what it takes to voluntarily damn oneself. We spent a good part of the afternoon and evening at the bar. He explained to me that he'd taken this path four years earlier, and that I was the first "colleague" he'd had the pleasure of meeting. His enthusiasm struck me as genuine, as if learning of my existence had lifted him out of a life of solitude. It probably had, in fact.

He shared his experience with me, proving to be very knowledgeable about the customs of our profession. He also knew an infinite number of details about the Brotherhood, although he'd never had the opportunity to meet any of its representatives. Like me, he always received his instructions through dream channels...

That day, we agreed on the undeniable existence of magic. It had been obvious all along, but I'd never really formulated it so clearly: we're the human arm of the magical expression of something more powerful than ourselves. How else can we explain the spontaneous appearance of a tattoo, the detailed instructions via our unconscious, and the apparent benefits of our work?

On this last point, of course, we have no irrefutable proof that it actually works, but we have to believe it does, for the sake of our dearly departed.

Eltz

16

Believ

I wake up feeling terribly hungover. I've barely slept at all; just enough to feel disoriented, not enough to be truly rested. My shoulder is gently shaken. I haven't opened my eyes yet.

"Believ, it's time."

That voice... Ah, my ghost is around. Good news. My heart reacts strangely to hearing him, setting a rapid pace that makes me nervous. I try not to pay too much attention to it, but I can't totally ignore the feeling of well-being I get from knowing he's nearby. I snort, trying to shake off the after-effects of drowsiness. I lift an eyelid, taking in the handsome man standing in front of me.

"I didn't see much," he tells me.

Nevertheless, he hands me a lantern he must have found among the monks. This simple gesture seems to exhaust him, which is hardly surprising if he's been lugging it around the abbey to bring it back to me. But it's not just that; he's agitated.

"The place emanates a sort of... repulsive aura," he concludes after a moment's reflection.

"Repulsive? As if the monks are aware of the existence of ghosts and guard against them?"

"Something like that."

This sucks! I thought the story could be settled; if not simply, then at least quickly, but now I know I was wrong.

"Please follow me."

He's definitely a bit bossy for a dead guy. Do I mind? Considering where we are and how insecure I am, I comply without flinching. We walk through two icy corridors and up stone staircases. When we reach the first floor, he goes off on a tangent.

"I'm going this way," he tells me as we leave the building to go into the cloister that leads to the gardens and outdoor areas.

As I had feared, the premises are immense and the idea of completing the circuit in such a short space of time seems compromised. Come to think of it, the logical thing to do would be to dedicate the upper floors to the cells, where I have little chance of finding a body. I might as well concentrate my search on the common areas.

Determined to proceed methodically, I rush down the corridor and open the doors one by one. First the refectory, lined with antique wooden tables hollowed out by centuries of use and benches so frail that I doubt they'll be able to support the weight of healthy monks for much longer. I continue on to the kitchens, then two rooms dedicated to relaxation—obviously, we don't share the same definition of the term—and finally, visiting rooms so austere that they would make those in today's prisons pale in comparison. The monks can barely make out their visitors through the wide claustra. The paintings, on the other hand, are breathtakingly beautiful. Depicting the surroundings, they cover every centimeter of the room, right up to the ceiling.

The rooms are so minimalist that I have little to examine. So, I head for the end of the corridor, which heralds an important annex: the abbey cloister.

Here, the stone walls are no longer clad with wood from furniture but are now expertly crafted with a careful paneling that reminds me of solid oak.

I'm walking toward the main hall when I hear voices. Someone's coming! If I just stand here, I'll be discovered. Where can I hide in this bare corridor?

The footsteps are getting closer; I've got to take cover now!

I can make out a curtain in front of an alcove containing a statue in a sorry state. It's so bulky that it leaves me little room. I crawl into a recess and fold back the heavy curtain.

Holding my breath in the folds of the dusty curtain where I've taken refuge, I hear voices arguing.

“I don't think you appreciate the scale of the problem: the body isn’t decomposing! We've tried burning it, but it's indestructible!”

“You're making this up, my dear man. It’s impossible!”

“I can confirm: the body hasn't changed in over a week. You'd think he was asleep—”

“It's imperative to find out what's wrong and how to solve the problem. It can't just sit there!”

“Well, I know, but what to do?”

“You've got some good ones! How do you expect us to identify the problem? Everything has been done according to your instructions.”

“Even the Sin Eater?”

“Even the Sin Eater.”

I feel like I recognize that voice.

“Did you attend the ceremony?”

“Are you kidding? I have no desire to be damned! I simply showed her the way. She managed.”

So it was Sir Jones who welcomed me to the manor. But what role does he play in this affair?

“Her?”

"Yes. It was a young woman. I couldn't tell you more, I hardly looked at her. When she left, the bread and beer were gone, and the candles had burned out..."

"You showed such courage," replies the other voice in an ironic tone. "And what do we do now? We've got to get rid of Ember Crow, and that means the body!"

"What do you suggest?"

"You tell me; you're the paranormal specialist! It's a matter of public order, I remind you. Use your brains!"

"As you just pointed out, I'm a paranormal specialist. I can't invent a solution to a problem I know nothing about."

"So you're no use to us at all!"

They continue to argue without really finding a solution to their problems. Although I've heard enough to understand that it's my ghost's body that's at stake, I'm forced to remain hidden.

So, my deceased's name is Ember Crow. A strange and sweet name, both poetic and mysterious.

What could he have done to make them want to get rid of him so badly?

And by what miracle does his flesh not decompose like any other body?

I'm getting used to the idea that his spirit lives on somewhere, but I'm stunned by the physical effects of his spiritual survival. These men are equally astonished, even though one of them is a "paranormal specialist."

What kind of invention is this again?

Are there other magical manifestations in this world?

Could it be that the supernatural is more than just a few dead people and ghosts?

Quite apart from the existence of magic as such, I'm shocked that the Church should be involved in this kind of occult activity, since it has always formally condemned all forms of magic except that of its Savior. That's why, century after century, they have eliminated all opponents on the grounds of witchcraft. So how can they justify having a sorcerer in their ranks?

It's so hypocritical. It's like common politicians saying, “Do as I say, not as I do.” As always, there's a double standard and, of course, the rules are more restrictive for ordinary citizens than for those in power. It's despicable.

The voices rise again.

“Wake up, there's no time to procrastinate. This is an emergency!”

“I know, but what can we do?”

“Try everything you can. The body has to go! Now! You wouldn't want that Ember Crow devil to come back to life, would you?”

“Is that even possible?”

“Of course it is! Why do you think we use Sin Eaters? It's far from an entertaining whim; it's to put a stop to this kind of heresy!”

Silence now reigns.

I don't think they were expecting such revelations.

Nor was I, for that matter...

The Church, which claims to be on the hunt for Sin Eaters it accuses of sinning, would our their services?

And then, it would be possible to resuscitate? Really?

Questions race through my poor head. It's a lot of information all at once, and I've barely digested the previous material. Now I've reached the in-between stage: I'm stunned by what I'm discovering, but I don't know enough to grasp the events as a whole. I'm going to have to learn more without being spotted. It's becoming a habit.

Above all, I must find Ember and tell him what I've discovered. Where the hell is he now?!

This pleasant interlude soon came to an end. We each had a mission to complete and, of course, we had to part ways. We returned to our respective rooms at the stroke of midnight. I had trouble falling asleep. My mind was torn—torn apart, in fact!—between the relief of having met Christy and the despair of having to leave so soon someone who could have become a true friend. Leaving the room the next morning, before sunrise, I discovered a Kraft paper bag leaning against my door. Christy apparently wanted to keep in touch and had made sure he could, by giving me a state-of-the-art cell phone, complete with instructions on how to use it.

Browsing quickly, I discovered his number in the phone book and a freshly received SMS:

> **Chris**
> We'll be in touch.

It was succinct, but clear: he didn't want to cut ties any more than I did. A wave of warmth swept through my heart. I now had a friend to whom I could confide my doubts and sorrows, a little happiness that restored some small light to my dark life.

Eltz

17

Ember Crow

Out in the open, the pressure eases, but something oppressive remains. These people are clearly hostile to me, although I still don't understand why.

The layout of this fortress gives the impression of a small, self-sufficient medieval town. Vegetable gardens rub shoulders with garment workshops, an industrial bakery, and a cemetery as creepy as it is intriguing.

Perhaps that's the place to start. What better place to hide a body than in a cemetery?

Under the thin rays of moonlight, I thread my way between ancient tombs, their modest crosses crumbling over the centuries. Most of the family names have been at least partially erased. Although well-maintained, the headstones seem frozen, with no vegetation other than freshly mown grass. Only a few docile flowers encircle the pathways, along with the occasional tortured tree, now devoid of foliage. No superfluous decoration, no ostentatious signs, just rows of sober, impersonal graves.

I methodically walk the aisles to make sure I haven't missed anything. With the exception of the gardener, there's no sign of anyone having been here recently. So, to imagine that someone could have brought a body here and buried it in the last few days seems unlikely. There's no trace of mine, not even a clue to point me in the right direction.

Once again, I find myself back where I started, unable to understand the reasons for my demise.

Despite the heavy atmosphere emanating from these old stones, I can't make out much that betrays their involvement in the trafficking of human tissue. Where would these churchmen be working, if they were to accumulate abnormal remains over the years? And in whose interest would they do so? I doubt they're working for science...

If this had been an ordinary organ deal, such an isolated location might have been as much a geographical handicap as a perfect cover. But I can't find a heliport or any other means of getting back into the air. And without air transport, I don't see how they could meet the demand, given the short lead times.

It's not that.

But what is it then?

What's wrong with me and why the interest?

How many others before me have been used by these men of the cloth for a purpose that still eludes me? No matter how much I poke around, this place isn't ready to give up its secrets.

I've got to find Believ. Even if I doubt she's learned anything more, I've got to make sure she's all right and get her out of this place before daybreak and the monks swarm the corridors again.

Where on earth could she be?

Chest compressed, I pace the first-floor corridors trying to locate her. She's discreet, to say the least; she remains invisible.

No longer bothering to follow the path traced by the walls, I cross them in a straight line, barely glancing into the rooms on either side of my route.

Believ, where are you?

This place oppresses me and alters my perception. My skull hurts as if my brain were trying to ooze out through my ears. If she were in the middle of the corridor, I wouldn't be able to see her anymore. I try to concentrate on the bond between us, the one I established the day I met her. In this place, it's tenuous, but still there. Like a safety line, I cling to it and, blindly, follow it to reach the one who will save me.

Every step is an ordeal, every breath brings a terrible burn. I pull myself up with difficulty, driven only by the fierce desire to find her before deserting this cursed place. As for my body, we'll find a solution that doesn't involve merging into these corridors.

Suddenly, a surge of pain assails me. My insides twist; I fall to my knees, unable to move. Paralyzed, I pass out.

It's been a while since I met
Christy. We still keep in touch by
phone. It's simple. I only have one
registered contact and I only use this
line when absolutely necessary, which is
never—until now. So I limit myself to
exchanging the odd text message with my
new friend. We're careful not to give each
other too much information and, above all,
never to reveal exactly where we stand. This
is a rule imposed by Christy; it took me
a while to understand it. At first, I
thought he was a little paranoid—but
then, who wouldn't be in such
circumstances?—and mocked him a

little, though I respected his instructions all the same. Who could wish us so much harm? I'm well aware that people don't really like us —not to say dislike us outright—because they're so afraid of us. Most of them believe that we're jinxed, that it's best to avoid us or, failing that, not to set eyes on us or meet our gaze.

But to physically assault us?

For a long time, it was hard to imagine. I never really raised the subject with my friend, preferring to confine myself to mild teasing. I dreaded discovering that the only person I could still confide in lacked discernment, or was even totally mad.

Eltz

18

Believ

I barely manage to stifle a scream of terror but let out a ragged breath that reverberates through the corridor.

Something just moved the curtain!

Hold your breath. Hold your breath.

How could someone come this way and I didn't hear them move? Are they levitating or something?

I can't go back any farther, compressed between the wall and an impassive Virgin. If someone draws the curtain, I'll be discovered.

Please, let him go on his way. Make him...

You would have to be pretty desperate to say a prayer that has no chance of being heard!

I don't even have time to finish my sentence when a shiver goes through me. Or rather, my stiff, who collapses *lifeless* through me.

Damn, he doesn't look good...

“Ember!” I call out to him, in a rather indiscreet whispered shout.

How can he understand that I'm talking to him? He doesn't even know his name!

“The ghost!”

And if not, does anyone have a mouth-to-mouth or cardiac massage method for spectra? What's happening to him?

"Ember. Your name is Ember Crow," I stammer, hoping my words will reach him despite his apparent unconsciousness.

He gradually comes to and emits a grunt of discomfort.

"Are you all right?"

"Wonderful!" he scoffs in a quavering voice. "We have to leave now."

"We have to stay!" I protest a little too loudly. "I got the confirmation we came for, Ember. You've been tricked! I don't know why, but the members of this order are trying to make you disappear."

"Ember..."

A strange gleam crosses his pupils, as if the mere mention of his name is enough to revive a part of his memory.

"Do you remember?"

"I remember the name, but I can't quite associate it with myself."

I imagine that amnesia is hard to live with and must, at times, have an aftertaste of schizophrenia.

"And that's not all. Not only is your body not deteriorating as it should, but it looks like you have the means to resuscitate!"

He writhes before me, tested by a spell that has no effect on me. If he can't move, how can we find his remains and bring him back to life?

"I'll take you back to the tunnel. I'll investigate on my own and come back for you when I've found something."

"Believ... It's too dangerous."

"How do you intend to proceed? You're not going to drag yourself through the corridors. You're going to..."

What, in fact? Technically, he's already dead...

"I refuse to let you suffer when there's another option. Just stay there."

He seems to consider the question but remains silent. It's never easy for a man to rely on a woman. The fact that I'm a Sin Eater makes no difference. Unable to support him physically, I offer encouragement, while trying to remember the way back to the tunnel. This building is a labyrinth, especially the basements, which seem to spread out even farther than the abbey above ground.

From alcoves to nooks and crannies, we reach the passageway that conceals our exit door. Now that I've wandered these corridors a little, I realize that it's just like the dozens of others that line this place.

"Wait for me here, and I'll come back for you. Do you understand me?"

Ember, who seems to have regained his composure, responds with an annoyed grunt.

"I won't be long."

I don't know why I feel the need to justify myself and brood over him. I agree that he's dead, but I'm not responsible for his fate. I can't help it, as if his future now depended on mine.

Before walking away, I grab the Swiss Army knife-shaped key-ring where the key to my motorcycle hangs and trace a small cross in the bottom of the door, a discreet way of distinguishing it at a glance in case of emergency. I've hardly taken a few steps when my heart sinks. What if I fail? What will happen if the monks succeed in destroying his body? Will he disappear with it?

I slip into the still deserted corridors, taut as a string, on the lookout for the slightest noise that might betray a presence. For the moment, the monks are still asleep, but for how much longer? As far as I know, they're the kind of people who get up before the sun. But from where I'm standing, it's impossible to see the slightest ray of it. And, of course, I don't have a watch handy.

Suddenly, I freeze. Footsteps sound on the cobblestones. I brace myself against the wall and move away as they approach, accompanied by a flickering light: a lantern. Really? Couldn't they have installed electricity? That said, it's picturesque and immersive, a surprising return to the roots of my profession.

A door opens.

I venture a peek, hoping to detect a clue to the visitor's destination. What I see stuns me: a dozen men are lined up in front of the door. One by one, they step inside after uttering what I imagine to be a password. The appearance of the last of them catches my eye: like me, he's dressed in an ordinary leather outfit for a biker. But that's not all! From his neck to the back of his skull unfurls an undulating tattoo: the mark of the Sin Eaters!

What's he doing here? Why go undercover like that and take such ill-considered risks? He's walking into the lion's den here!

When the door closes, I move closer. I've got to find out what's going on here!

One morning, however, reality hit me in the face, and I realized that Christy hadn't exaggerated the threat. I arrived on the outskirts of a village where I was planning to officiate, when I spotted the remains of a man hanging from a tree. I approached, slowing down my motorcycle. It was so improbable that at first I thought it was a kid's prank, but it wasn't Halloween. The realism of this horror sent shivers down my spine. Blood was still dripping, forming a scarlet stain on the grass at the corpse's feet. A few birds were circling the remains, probably disturbed by my presence. It was real.

There was a poor man, savagely butchered before being exposed, in tatters, for passers-by to see. Barbarism, pure and simple. I was so absorbed in contemplating this horror that I didn't hear a young boy come up beside me. He gently tapped my elbow to attract my attention. The apparent indifference of his boyish face surprised me. He was neither shocked nor disgusted by this atrocious spectacle. "Gross, huh?" he asked. "It's monstrous, yes," I replied, retching. I'd become accustomed to finding myself in the presence of lifeless bodies, but this one was just too bloody. "You don't seem surprised... Does that happen often around here?"

"It happens... They just have to stay home!

Don't invade us! Because of people like him, the Lord could condemn us!"

"The Lord?"

"Well, God!"

"But what could he have done to deserve such a sanction?"

He thought he was Christ..."

"I don't get it."

He's a Sin Eater! Look, his tattoo's hanging right there."

He then pointed to a piece of skin that had turned brown, a waving dragon still visible beneath the barely dried blood.

Shocked by the relentlessness to which this body had been subjected, I hadn't noticed the flap on display on the tree, pinned up like a poster. An unambiguous warning to Sin Eaters, apparently. The message got through. I turned back, even if it meant abandoning a poor dead man to his fate. All his family had to do was help him.

Eltz

19

Believ

I'm pacing up and down the wall, determined to find a way in, or at least catch whatever is being said in this room.

No matter how hard I try to keep a low profile, I can't completely hide my footsteps. My heels keep clicking on the stone floor. A kind of echo bounces from wall to wall, amplifying the signs of my passage. Eventually, it'll give me away. I have no choice: I take off my sneakers, tie the laces together, and slip them around my neck. I find myself in my socks on the shiny flagstones, made slippery by wear and tear.

I scan the hallway until I hear the sound of voices. If they're shouting like that, maybe standing behind the door will be enough to let me hear this unsettling exchange. I press my ear against the door and hold my breath. The shouting continues, but I can't make out what's being said.

The sheer volume of the clamor makes me realize, however, that this isn't a conversation between a handful of men. I'm afraid the entire chapter of monks is here! Why such a gathering? Who are these people who have come to meet the monks? And why is this audience being held in a remote basement room?

The most important thing is to avoid being noticed. I place my hand on the handle and turn it slowly, before carefully opening the door. I slide my head into the gap and discover that it's an amphitheater. Monks and visitors are chatting loudly below.

As I enter the huge hall where the debate is taking place, an intense thrill runs through me. I feel as if I'm witnessing a major event; not just for me, but for humanity.

My presence has never been so discreet. I sneak up behind the last seats, close to the door I leave ajar, and stare at this strange spectacle I never thought I would witness. I can now clearly hear this surreal exchange:

"With all due respect, your Brotherhood only exists because we tolerate it! You must submit to our rules and our will!"

That voice! I recognize it; it's one of those I heard earlier last night!

What brotherhood is he talking about? How many of them gravitate to the shadows?

I'm lost in conjecture before plunging back into the lively debate below.

"I hear you, Your Lordship, and you know perfectly well that we've been at it for centuries now. But this is too much! We can't go on like this. We refuse to—"

"What do you mean, you refuse? When did you think we were asking for your opinion?"

"That's enough of that! You don't have to address us in that tone of voice! You run your Church, I run my Brotherhood; to each his cross!"

"You don't understand! Your Brotherhood only exists because we created it. And why do you think we did it? Because it's useful to us!"

"You've taught me nothing. We understand perfectly well that our services serve your cause. Otherwise, why do you insist on them so insistently?"

"Unfortunately, I don't think you understand everything. You're not just here to assist us, you're an integral part of our institution. A subsidiary, of sorts."

"How so?"

The man who appears to be the Brotherhood's leader chokes on his words. He's clearly outraged by what he has just learned.

"Obviously, you didn't think the Church would risk getting its hands dirty or being double-crossed. The Sin Eaters Brotherhood was created centuries ago precisely to avoid this kind of unpleasantness."

The Sin Eaters Brotherhood!

Is the Sin Eaters Brotherhood an arm of the Church? It can't be!

And what have I got to do with it?

What's my role?

"You look surprised. Did you really not know?"

Those I now guess to be Sin Eaters remain mute, stunned. So the one I spotted when they arrived isn't an infiltrator, but an unofficial guest!

"Let me tell you the story in more detail. To get to the point... A few centuries ago, faith in the Church was declining so dangerously—to the benefit of belief in magic—that we had to act to halt this predicted decline. We were forced to kill two birds with one stone: exterminate magic at any cost and frighten the population to keep it under the yoke of the Church. However, we had no effective means of doing so, despite the presence of sorcerers devoted to our cause—yes, I know, it's paradoxical, but as long as everyone gets something out of it, there's no need to be too fussy—and we weren't in a position to get rid of magical beings once and for all."

Magic? There are sorcerers in the pay of the Church! Like that supernaturalist who took me in at Sir Jones's...

"That's where the Sin Eaters came in," he continues, clearly delighted to unpack this crucial information. "Under the guise of offering forgiveness to the dead, you have enabled us to banish thousands of magical beings from this dimension once and for all. As far as humans are concerned, your intervention has only minimal effects, but it does have a significant psychological influence. The Sin Eaters, therefore, play an essential role in our supremacy. To establish our dominance, we had to be sure that your office would be assured at all times. And what better way to do this than to forbid the use of your services?"

I'm stunned. My colleagues are too, judging by their posturing, even though they clearly knew that the Church's condemnation of us was merely a facade designed not to tarnish its already crumbling reputation. By giving our lives and our souls, we believed we were doing a good deed, working on the right side, even if it never occurred to me to imagine the Church playing on the wrong side.

In truth, we were the playthings of higher authorities, destined to control citizens in spite of ourselves and turn them into docile sheep, frightened by a radical sentence.

The Master of the Brotherhood finally intervenes.

"I don't understand how you could have hidden such a thing from us. Our books would have mentioned it. It can't be true. You're lying!"

"Let's just say we didn't leave anything to chance. Once your Brotherhood was up and running, we erased its genesis to make sure it functioned perfectly. The first person to play your role was captured before we could reveal the inner workings of our collaboration. How could you have played the game of the desperate faithful if you didn't believe in this divine ban yourselves?"

"And the sacrificed Sin Eaters?" he asks feverishly.

"In the beginning, we were involved. It was necessary to make this prohibition as tangible as possible. Our faithful needed to know that sins could only be absolved by God Himself, and that any other means would be perilous. In this way, the practice could remain confidential and have the desired effect."

"What are the expected effects?"

"I told you: the annihilation of all magic that does not emanate from our Lord!"

"How can we be responsible for the disappearance of magic? As you know, we use it to recruit our members..."

"That was the subtlety of this manipulation. We don't mind what you do with it. On the other hand, it was necessary to erase its existence from the minds of ordinary mortals. How can you ensure your power over someone who is convinced that magic will come to their rescue? Thanks to you, uncontrolled magical manifestations have been reduced over time, and with them, beliefs. Confronted with the harshness of reality, people have turned in abundance to faith, the only magic still 'tolerated.' And that's where the mass effect comes in."

"But what does it actually do for you?"

"Everything! At the time, cash flow was at its worst, and people no longer wished to finance the Church. All this was necessary to remobilize them and assure us of their devotion to our cause. To us, in short!"

"But how can you, who preach humanity, solidarity, and love, condone such a scheme? You're abusing these poor people for your own individualistic ends, sanctioned by your own rules!"

"You mean this old book," mocks the monk, pointing with a dismissive gesture to a scratched Bible lying not far from him. "You know, if there's one thing history—and Nebuchadnezzar, in particular—has taught us, it's that rules are best respected when they're written down. The trick is to wrap them up nice and tidy to get the message across. Then it's just a matter of repeating them and inviting the faithful to immerse themselves in them in their spare time."

When he finishes his sentence, a heavy silence settles in place of the heated debate, somewhere between amazement and protest. No one really knows how to react, whether it's the Sin Eaters or the brothers, some of whom are also stunned.

This unpacking is ill-timed, yet the man from whom it emanates has a huge smile on his face. A terrifying smile. I'm sure he wouldn't be so arrogant if he didn't still have some cards up his sleeve. In fact, if he's admitting all this, it's probably because he's several moves ahead and is certain to win.

A member of the Brotherhood in his thirties, visibly preoccupied, shyly speaks up.

"How could we have participated in such things without realizing it? Personally, I've never seen or even glimpsed a magical creature."

"That's the genius of our organization, young man. If you think you've never seen one, it's only because we've concealed them from your eyes with a crude enchantment. You were so convinced that you were working for the good of others, in accordance with your conscience, that a simple transformation spell was enough to fool you as to the appearance of the deceased to whom you were offering your services."

"A transformation spell..." he murmurs, incredulous.

"Absolutely. What word have you missed in what I've just told you? Although you seem convinced of the contrary, you are superficial beings, more attached to appearance than to the heart. Deceiving you was child's play. In fact, that's the mission entrusted to our guild..."

He then lets out a Machiavellian laugh.

I'm afraid I understand: so even I, who is just discovering the original scope of magic, have contributed to its extinction?

Does my meeting with Ember have any particular meaning in this centuries-old plot?

Does he belong to the community of magical creatures whose appearance has been masked? Could he be a victim of this genocide?

After this incident, I rode for a long time before stopping again. I was shocked. How could someone be punished for helping others? Wasn't the sacrifice of a life and eternal damnation enough? Was it really necessary to impose so much suffering on someone so devoted? I was revolted. It was profoundly unfair. And nothing shakes me more than injustice. Haunted by the images of this poor colleague and unable to calm myself, I called Christy. I had to understand the reasons for such carnage if I was to ease my anguish.

My friend picked up the phone in a panic.

"Eltz, what's wrong? Is everything okay?"

The words stuck in my throat. After a long silence, I asked him, "Why do Sin Eaters have to hide, Christy? Why? To protect themselves from whom? From what?"

I heard him swallow with difficulty. My questions must have taken him by surprise.

"You're not really ignorant of the answer to that, are you? It's the Church that's out to get us... You know what the clergy claim?"

"No. I don't know anything about it."

"They claim that in freeing people from their sins,

we're guilty of the sin of pride. As if we were claiming to have the powers of Christ. That's why we shouldn't be paid more than six coins..."

"And that gives them the right to kil l us like dogs and expose our bodies to popular vindictiveness? It's unworthy of God's representatives! It's a service we render to the community at the cost of our very existence. Can't they see that?"

"I know... The price is even higher than you imagined, isn't it?"

I was furious.

I hadn't imagined for a second that the reprisals would take on such proportions, but I refuse to give in to fear. No! They won't make me give in to panic or abandon my mission. I've chosen this path out of conviction, and I'll honor my commitment. It's a question of honor. And maybe even pride, after all.

I know, however, that from now on I'll have to be even more cautious, as furtive as the ghosts I free from their wanderings.

Eltz

20

Ember

After a few minutes in the underground passage, I feel less feverish, although the unpleasant tingling persists. The distance between the hall of worship and me certainly has something to do with it.

How did these people know that the dead could enter these walls? There's no answer to this question—this simple spell alone proves that these monks aren't what they seem! If they protect themselves from specters, it's because they're involved in many deaths. And most likely in mine...

Now that I've come to my senses, I'm feeling a little apprehensive. Where has Believ gone? Why isn't she back?

I can't quite grasp the rhythm of time, so I don't know whether she left me a few minutes or several hours ago. And all this for what? To find a body that I can no longer inhabit, at the risk of losing her own life!

This reality hits me hard. Why would she make such a sacrifice when I'm already dead? It just doesn't make sense.

I must find her and rescue her from the clutches of these unscrupulous monks!

I leave the underground passage and enter the suffocating basement. A strange atmosphere reigns here, a heavy feeling that creeps over me in addition to the horrible sensation resulting from the protection spell.

Where do I go from here?

I re-attach myself to the bond with Believ, the one I mentally forged when we first met, and make my way through the gleaming stone corridors.

Soon there is a rumbling sound, preceded by sharp, peremptory words.

“You're no longer the leader this Brotherhood needs,” thunders a voice. “And if you're not, you don't belong here!”

A wave of protest breaks out.

Those to whom these words are addressed are clearly outraged at being sidelined in this way.

I enter the room and feel Believ's presence. She's no longer here, but she has been here.

“Brother David. Your turn.”

Though calmly pronounced, these words have the effect of a cleaver. The room falls silent. And before I know what they mean, one of the monks pulls a gun from the belt of his habit and, without the slightest hesitation, shoots the man standing in front of him.

The victim collapses without a word. There isn’t a sound to disturb the silence of the audience, only the imperceptible rustling of the fabric of his clothes and the dull thump of his body on the parquet floor of the podium.

His supporters are dumbfounded, frozen in front of the monks who adopt the triumphant posture of vile conquerors.

“You!” commands the giver of orders. “Step right up.”

A blond man in his forties takes a few halting steps. Now that he stands out from the mass of his peers, I can make out a strange tattoo on his arm that reminds me of something. Where have I seen this before?

“By the powers of the Holy Church vested in me, I appoint you as the successor. You will be the new Guide of this Brotherhood.”

"Me?" he wonders aloud. "I'm just another Sin Eater, Your Holiness."

What a pompous title!

The other sweeps his words aside with a dismissive gesture.

"Now you know what risks you run if your order deviates from the mission we've assigned it, don't you?"

The blond nods, jaw clenched.

"So I have no doubt you'll keep it on track." A perverse smile stretches across his face. How can a religious man be so full of deceit?

"I'll do my best," confirms the blond man, miming a low bow.

"I know you will."

Once again, silence spreads through the room with the speed of a pandemic. There's nothing serene about it; the things left unsaid overwhelm it, and so does the tension.

I got caught up in what's going on here, but I don't care what happens to these people. And if they're enough of a distraction to take attention away from Believ, then all the better.

I leave the room without a backward glance and go back in search of the one who haunts my mind.

If through any fault of mine something were to happen to her, I wouldn't survive it...

Despite the obstacles, I continue my quest. I travel from town to town, visiting the dead and their families. I'm adding ever more precautions to my protocol, to make sure I don't end up like the unfortunate Sin Eaters who stain my landscape. For holy men, those of the clergy have no shortage of imagination and a keen sense of torture. With each macabre discovery, I appreciate a little more the sadism of these wolves in sheep's clothing.

Eltz

21

Believ

The basement is as immense as the abbey that conceals it. Perhaps even more so. And I haven't visited a quarter of it.

Once I'm far enough away from the amphitheater, I slip on my shoes and tighten them as much as I can. In this way, I hope to reduce the echo of my footsteps on the slippery slabs without risking a fall.

By the light of Ember's lantern, I hurry along, poking my head in at every door I come across, to establish a sort of mental map of the place in case I have to come back. Given the time available, it's more than likely that I'll have to walk these icy corridors again, even if I would prefer not to.

Rhythmic footsteps approach. I have just enough time to duck behind a door and watch a handful of silent monks pass by. I imagine that the night is drawing to a close and that soon there will be so many of them that I won't be able to avoid them.

Now that I know they have cold-blooded killers in their ranks, the prospect of running into them is nipping at my heels. Since they've been eliminating our own since the dawn of time to preserve the secrecy of their hold, how many of them are ready to eliminate an unwelcome Sin Eater without batting an eye? My situation is like a kind of Russian roulette: at any moment, I could find myself face to face with a devoted lamb or a determined executioner. I would much rather not play.

When silence returns, I slip out of my hiding place and dart down the corridor. I have to finish my scouting as quickly as possible. I tiptoe along, keeping to the shadows, my hard-shelled rucksack as protection. Cells follow work and prayer rooms, and I feel as if I've traveled back in time to an unenviable medieval past. There's no trace of modern comfort; not even electricity in most of the rooms.

Suddenly, I change dimensions. A rusted metal grate stands in the middle of the corridor, between two forks. Behind it, the path continues in darkness. What is it trying to protect? How do I get past it?

Above the passageway, a tightly packed row of strange gargoyles stare at me with piercing eyes. Do they mark the entrance to the catacombs? To the crypt? The mere fact that this passageway is restricted is enough to arouse my curiosity. What I'm looking for is probably there, but how do I get in?

I grasp the cold, rusty bars and shake the door, torn between urgency and the need to make no sound that would betray my presence. It barely moves. And yet, no matter how hard I inspect it, I can't find a lock or any mechanism designed to open it. At the same time, if an access pass had to be distributed to each religious person authorized to cross this junction, a mountain of keys would have been needed. There's got to be a way, I'm sure!

"So, girls, what's the secret?" I murmur, my eyes fixed on the motionless gargoyles.

"What secret?"

I jump. As if I'd been expecting an answer! Who is it? I can't make out anyone, especially as I hastily turned off my lantern at the sound of the voice.

What to do?

I have nowhere to escape and nowhere to hide. I have to face it.

"The one that opens this door," I whisper, my breathing suspended.

"Ah, that one! Just—"

My interlocutor, still invisible, doesn't have time to finish his sentence before a flock of religious people rush into a nearby corridor.

"There's someone on this side!"

A movement grazes me, both light and powerful. This guy's no light-weight! In a matter of seconds, even though we're still in the dark, I hear the gate open.

How did he do it?

"Go ahead, I'll catch up."

Although his manner surprises me and his motivation remains obscure, I don't hesitate and rush into the passage, taking care to close the gate. Absorbed by the darkness, I press on, my hand glued to the wall. It's only when I hear nothing more that I stop to catch my breath.

Where does this endless corridor lead? How come nobody tried to chase me? Have I actually gone unnoticed? Could this stranger have saved my ass?

After making sure I'm alone, I turn on my lantern and take in the surroundings. I'm in a stone tunnel, similar to those I've already visited, except that there are no doors along its smooth walls. There's obviously only one destination, which must be at the end of the tunnel.

A shiver runs through me.

Either I find what I'm looking for, or I'm done in like a rat. Maybe even both, who knows?

Although the outcome of this mission has never been in doubt, I'm struck by the prospect of a fatal result. Even if I find Ember's body, my story ends here. For good. Without ever again being able to see the one for whom I've made all these sacrifices. My love, my son: Lewis.

I tremble from head to toe, remembering the moments of fulfillment spent by his side; the same ones that come back to me every night before turning into unbearable nightmares. How happy I was to have him with me! He was a ray of sunshine in the winter of my life. Thanks to him, I'd had no trouble overcoming his father's abandonment, even though he had been the main cause.

We were both happy, until it was ripped away from me.

I had hoped one day to find him, but now I know that it will only be after his death—which I hope will be a long time off—that we will be reunited. Not before. We won't share anything while we're still alive. I won't be the support I had hoped to be for him. Never again.

I'm not even sure right now that he's okay. What if I've been chasing fantasies all this time? What if he's already gone, and my impending death brings us together, without further ado?

I'm rambling, shaking with tremors that could be the result of so many factors: fear, cold, lack...

I'll have the answers to my questions soon enough.

I take a deep breath, shake out my stiffened muscles, and sink into the gloom, swallowed by cold and nothingness. My heart beats between my ears, and I'm aware that this is where it all hangs out. Not my inevitable end, but Ember's fate, and probably that of the magic of our world.

The magic...

To think I had believed it was confined to a few divine mission orders. It was so simplistic and so far from reality! If only I had been able to grasp its scope and enjoy its virtues. Once again, the truth comes too late.

After an uncertain time, a bright light appears in the darkness of the tunnel. The end is nigh.

Although anxious, I press on. The sensation of leaving my body and becoming a spectator of what's happening to me grips me. It's as if I'm in the middle of a cottony cloud, guiding my steps from a distance.

I enter an immense dome which, although underground, is strangely luminous. Frozen on the threshold, I observe the stone vault, covered with a luminescent material that radiates with such vigor that it's as if the place were bathed in daylight.

Rows of metal tables follow rows of metal tables, and on one wall, silver death chests, typical of a classic morgue. The image of the police morgue comes back to me. It was ridiculously cramped compared to the facility opposite me. Here, the refrigerated compartments run right up to the ceiling. A kind of forklift, designed to convey the remains, is parked at the bottom of the wall.

How many bodies can they store here?

Is it necessary to keep so many at the same time? What is the reason for this? Why here?

"We have orders to try everything," says a voice hidden behind an opaque screen.

"What else can we try?"

Crouching down, I discreetly step forward to try and catch a snatch of what they're talking about.

"Let's recap," begins the first voice, accompanied by the sound of crumpling paper. "According to Brother Stefan's notes, the body has undergone no natural alterations since death. The flesh has remained intact and firm, barely discolored, suggesting that its owner still inhabits it."

"But he's really dead!"

"Of course he's dead; that's the point of the spell! Well, almost..."

What does he mean, "almost"?

Is this guy dead or not?

"We need to start from the beginning to understand what makes this case different from the others."

"His identity, perhaps?"

"I doubt that's enough."

"After all, this is Ember Crow we're talking about! Not just any magical creature, he's—"

"That's enough of this! Never speak his name again! He's dead!"

"If you say so..." He frowns.

So it's my ghost they're so worried about?

"As I was saying," resumes the first, whose voice betrays his annoyance, "his body remained frozen in a state similar to a simple sleep. However, the body was studied and then cremated, as required by procedure. Nevertheless, it refused to be consumed."

"You mean it didn't burn when placed in the crematorium? Do you think his particular nature would have interfered with the process?"

Couldn't he be more specific with his thoughts? What exactly does "his nature" refer to? How can I understand what's going on if I only have bits and pieces of information?

In any case, it confirms one thing: Ember is a magical creature, despite his ordinary appearance. As to which one, it's impossible to say, especially as I don't know which species really exist. However, I find it hard to imagine him as a fairy or a korrigan. A kelpie perhaps?

I suppress a giggle. No, really, my stiff doesn't look the part. At the same time, I have no idea what he really looks like, which doesn't help me in my speculations.

I continue to make progress toward the forensic team, in the hope of finally discovering what happened to Ember and, above all, how to reverse the effects.

"How should I know?" demands the first voice.

"Let's go back over the chronology," suggests the one I imagine to be an assistant.

"Let's hear it."

"According to the report, the squadron lured our subject into an ambush, immobilized him, froze his gifts, and cast the death spell on him."

"That's it." The first nods, taut as a string. "Three spells in a row."

How can anyone remain so calm in the face of such a violent enumeration? Ember was framed and murdered!

"Stripped of his psyche and magic, a prisoner of our world, his body, which had adopted its human form for the encounter, remained captive. Strange. I'd have thought his flesh would have spontaneously turned into... you know."

"It's a step I can't quite explain myself, to tell you the truth. Not all creatures are shapeshifters, you know. For some, a transformation spell is required to subject them to the—"

"Sin Eaters. I was just getting to that. The report is silent on the subject. Do you know more?"

"The Brotherhood commissioned one of its own. A woman, if I understood correctly."

"So, he was freed of his sins, transported to the morgue, and returned to the abbey. Is this correct?"

"Absolutely. Nothing abnormal, then."

"Nothing. And yet, the situation suffices to demonstrate the contrary."

They fall silent for a moment.

"Do you believe he's still here?" the assistant asks thoughtfully.

"I don't believe anything. This situation is completely beyond me. With the exception of the state of his remains, there's nothing to indicate that the procedure failed. In fact, there's every reason to believe that it had the desired effect. That said, we mustn't discount this hypothesis, as he could well be out there..."

"How have we managed to keep him away from his body so far?"

"Like the abbey, his body is protected by a repulsive enchantment, materialized by these blessed stones. Perhaps, in his case, this is what is interfering with his firm and definitive death."

"But if I follow your demonstration, if we take them off, he's liable to repossess it! So there's no way we can't use them!" rages the young monk, suddenly frightened.

"I'm afraid we've reached a dead end..."

So much the better!

I keep moving forward, but just as I'm about to duck behind a cupboard, I stumble. To avoid crashing headfirst into the doors, I hold out my hands. I escape mashing my brain but fail to conceal my fall against the metal panels, which resonate under the dome, alerting the forensic monks, whom I hear leaping simultaneously from their armchairs.

"Sound the alarm!"

After the hanging shreds, I came across a charred body in its car, its bloody tattoo exposed on the asphalt just ahead. Then it was the turn of the crucified man on a bridge, the decapitated man sitting on a park bench—charming, by the way—and, finally, the suicidal man thrown from a building who crashed at my feet. What they all had in common was that they all died horrific deaths. What's more, their tattoos had been ripped from their arms and put on display, like a signature. An unambiguous warning.

What's even more astonishing is that these abominable acts have never been mentioned in the media, and that law enforcement agencies don't seem to be any the wiser.

Presumably, they were asked to turn a blind eye to these few specific cases. It's reassuring to know that we're protected by corrupt police officers who can be bought for a handful of euros or a few grams of drugs, as the case may be.

It doesn't really surprise me. I've never really liked these people, most of whom delight in abusing what little power they have. With each new body,

I'm off like the wind, without a second thought.

I always fear that the sponsors are still on site, precisely to observe the demonstrations of any sympathizers.

Eltz

22

Ember

The more I find out about what's going on here, the more my anxiety grows and with it, the dull fear of losing Believ. Just thinking about it makes my chest feel painfully tight.

Leaving the clandestine conclave behind me, I follow the Sin Eater's trail through the corridors, making no further attempt to conceal my presence.

I feel I'm getting closer to her. It's as if her aura exerts a magnetic attraction that guides me without me even having to check. But when I arrive like a tornado in one of the corridors, it's not her who appears to me, but a group of monks chatting with a man whose appearance reminds me of those in the amphitheater.

“I'm telling you, I got lost looking for the amenities!”

“But this isn't your first meeting, Christy.”

Christy... The name rings a bell. Would I have known him in some unattainable past?

“Forgive me, but these corridors, really. Who wouldn't get lost? It’s a veritable maze!”

“What were you looking for?”

"What was I... But you're completely delirious; I just have to pee! And if you hold my leg like that, I'll have to relieve myself against the wall..."

"Seriously? Hold on!"

"So, the latrines?" insists Christy before the stunned eyes of the monks, who are disconcerted to see him holding so firmly to his lies.

"Please follow me."

"Then you'll be accountable."

"Anything, as long as I can empty my bladder without waiting another quarter of an hour!"

The small group moves away, revealing a passageway that their presence had hitherto concealed. Enclosed by a grate, it displays nothing but eternal night. Yet this is where my instincts tell me to go. And the longer I procrastinate, the more my intuition leads me to believe that whoever got pinched a few seconds ago pointed Believ in this direction.

Has he set a trap for her?

More than likely, for what obscure reason would he have wanted to fly to her rescue? And by what miracle would he have found himself face to face with her in this unlikely place?

I break through the bars and float as fast as I can. But as I advance, I feel the effects of the spell that had struck me down two floors up. Weakened, my progress becomes slower and more difficult. Impalpable, I have no means of holding on, no support other than my determination to find Believ, whose confusion and apprehension surround me even though she's no longer present within these walls.

Believ, where are you?

I continue my levitation and pick up the pace. Suddenly, a thud sounds before bouncing down the corridor, followed by hysterical screams.

"Sound the alarm!"

"Don't touch me!"

These are the protests of the one I'm looking for! Her voice—though wheezy—has never sounded so sweet to me. She's all right.

For now.

Despite the pain, I rush down the corridor. After interminable seconds, I emerge under a luminescent dome, where the monks seem to have combined a morgue and a laboratory. It doesn't take a great deal of thought to realize that they've been experimenting on the bodies of those they've suppressed. All in all, an irreproachable ethic and morality.

Suddenly, a folding screen collapses under the weight of a monk trying to escape Believ's assault. Despite her small stature, she leaps at the monk's throat without hesitation, punching him under the chin and in the ribs.

Hitherto content to carry out an invariable procedure, diligently reproducing the precepts she had been taught, she now indulges in majestic improvisation.

I can see the rage on her tired features. She deals out blows without even thinking about it, and she takes some too. But there's nothing fair about the fight: there are two of them. Two well-built, well-trained churchmen against a young woman barely thicker than a toothpick.

"Reinforcements are on the way!"

Reinforcements?

It doesn't help the situation. What does "reinforcements" mean? Two men? Ten men? Twenty?

She dodges a blow and, in one agile move, leaps over a body lying on an autopsy table.

My body.

It's obvious. I know it. No, I feel it as surely as if I were looking in a mirror.

As the monk moves around the table, she slips her hands into her pockets, as if to taunt him. Her eyes sparkle with rage and provocation. Yet she doesn't utter a word. She's wild, she's free. No god on Earth can impose his will on her, least of all one of his usurped representatives. That's what I admire about her. What I love, in addition to her sumptuous curves.

She grabs an object from a nearby shelf and throws it with all her might. Her pursuer deflects it with his broad arm. It falls without causing any damage other than the anger of the cleric, who pounces on her without further ado.

She pushes the cart with vigor, before running in the opposite direction. But she didn't count on the second monk, who intercepts her and holds her captive with his muscular arms.

"I've got her!"

"Ember!" she calls, her cry muffled by the grip that immobilizes her.

Fatal error.

He touched her.

He defiled Believ.

My Believ.

I'm going to kill him.

Despite these horrific murders, I've adopted a simple routine of moving every two weeks or so, according to my dreams and intuitions. Last night, however, I was contacted through a letter left under my hotel room door. Although I inspected the corridor, I couldn't see by which charitable soul it had been deposited. And despite my insistent requests, the manager stubbornly refused to allow me to view the surveillance cameras. Come to think of it, it's not even certain that they were ever connected to the recording system. Who the hell knows I'm here? Obviously,

I haven't told anyone, not even Christy. It's got to be a Brotherhood thing, that's all I can think of.

So, I carefully opened the missive and discovered its contents: an alarming newspaper article about a new, unexplained epidemic. The journalist points out, not without a good dose of pathos, that like the previous ones, this disease is totally unknown and there is no known cure, so the list of those who have succumbed to it is growing impressively. It appears to have set a record for mortality in the blink of an eye. Hardly reassuring. As I was inspecting the envelope, a small piece of paper fell out. It was a sort of Post-it note, on which was written an address and a surname. A very subtle way of assigning me my next mission.

So I left the hotel, without much regret given the mediocre quality of the facilities and service—at the same time, I couldn't reasonably expect high standards, given the state of my finances—and decided to head east. The target is nowhere near, and the journey seems interminable. My serenity has left me for good. I'm worried for my friend; for myself too. The feeling of being followed or observed never leaves me. It's probably not just a feeling, in fact... I thought Christy was paranoid until I was confronted with a slew of sacrifices: why shouldn't I be the next victim of these godless lunatics?

Eltz

23

Believ

"Don't let go!"

I struggle as best I can, gesticulating despite the grip tightening on my chest. How come all the monks in this abbey are bodybuilders? What's happened to the paunchy, flabby brothers we see on TV?

"Let go of me!"

My arms compressed against my chest, I can do nothing but throw my feet in all directions. The second monk comes to my captor's rescue. Even in his wildest dreams, he won't get his filthy hands on me! Despite the lack of air, I redouble my efforts and give him a well-felt kick right in the family jewels! He's got no use for them anyway!

"Ember!" I shout again, hoping my cry will cross the basement and reach him.

"Be quiet!"

"Is she really calling him?" exclaims the other, unsure of his understanding of the situation.

Delighted to see them unsettled, I continue.

"Ember! Ember!"

Just as the second comes charging back and is about to grab my ankles, he collapses as if he had hit something and knocked himself out.

Just in time!

Am I talking to myself or has my knight in shining armor come to my rescue? Since I can't see him, it's hard to say.

"It's me," he confirms, a smile in his voice.

Now my stiff is talking to me in my thoughts!

Taking advantage of the surprise caused by the chief pathologist's fall, I elbow the second monk in the stomach, and he immediately loosens his grip and lets me fall to the floor littered with dissecting instruments. I grab a scalpel and brandish it in front of me. This weapon is ridiculous, but if it can inflict even minor damage, it's worth it.

The coroner stares at me, poised on his feet, ready to parry any attack. If I lunge, he'll knock me off my feet. I wait. But for what? If reinforcements arrive before he attacks me, I lose any chance of escape. I need Ember.

"Ember!"

I'm... I'm coming!

Why the softened tone? Could it be that he's suffering from the same ailment as he did on the upper floors? He probably is. In fact, that's why I brought him back to the basement and told him to stay there. How did he reach me? Why did he do this?

My opponent's leg buckles at the knee. He crashes to the ground, surprised to see no one around.

Without dwelling on it, I take advantage of his confusion to flee. Which way? The only exit is also the one that will lead the reinforcements here. If I enter the corridor, I'm bound to run into them!

In the middle of a stride, I'm petrified. I won't have time to hide; a divine squadron stands before me. These men are monks in name only. Everything about their posture, facial expressions, and gestures betrays that they're authentic warriors. Modern-day crusaders, armed to the teeth—and not with unwieldy swords, but with cutting-edge weaponry that would be the envy of the British Army! Where did they get such an arsenal?

"See you there!"

I have no choice. I raise my hands above my head, even though there's no doubt about the outcome of this fateful day. Did Eltz know this was how it would end when he entrusted me with his succession? That I would be unable to honor his silent promise to save the soul of his daughter, Elsa?

In my trembling flesh, I feel Ember's discomfort writhing farther away. A fine pair of cripples we are. At least we'll perish together, united against adversity and against this Church that only preaches for its parish, to the detriment of universal magic.

"So it's you who's disturbing the serenity of our abbey, miss?"

I remain mute. There's no answer to this rhetorical question.

"Has the cat got your tongue?"

I spit on him; he doesn't even deserve my consideration. Upset that I'm resisting him, his skin takes on a red hue that makes him even uglier.

"That's the one! I recognize her!" exclaims a guy who clearly doesn't belong with the commandoes.

I recognize the voice I'm hearing for the third time in just a few days: that of the man who welcomed me to Sir Jones's manor! I imagine that, after his clandestine interview in the corridor in the middle of the night, he preferred to stay in the abbey rather than return home in a hurry. He's not done dragging us around yet, that idiot!

"Explain yourself, will you?"

"She's the one who worked with Ember Crow!"

"What have you done, my dear, for him to survive this way?"

"I won't say a word."

"As you please. But I doubt you'll appreciate the fate Brother Joshua has in store for you. Will she?" he asks, a perverse smile plastered on his mouth.

"I'm ready to intervene," Joshua confirms. "My tools are always ready."

The collusion between these two men is heavy with innuendo. It's downright creepy. And the mere anticipation of what he's about to inflict on me sends an unpleasant shiver down my spine, the harbinger of insurmountable pain. Never mind, I'm ready for Ember. For Lewis too. Ready to simply give my life a new meaning. I'm not a creature-killer. I'll never betray the weakest or the most destitute for the benefit of a materialistic congregation. My only master is freedom!

"Very well, then. Tie her up and take her away. You know where..."

His tone has softened. He no longer needs to impose himself with volume; he lets these few words hang in the air as if they were the death knell of my existence. In the end, it's what they suggest that's most eloquent. I'll end up in pieces, but I'll never give them any information. Ever. So, at least my integrity and honor are preserved, if not my conscience.

"Let's go!"

Everything is swirling.

Everything is so dazzlingly white!

Maybe not so much, in fact... Everything comes in shades of gray now.

I haven't left Earth; I'm still here.

Yet I remember I was on my way to my next mission when my bike went out of control. There was nothing I could do. I ended up in the scenery.

In my misfortune, I was lucky. Doubly so. I didn't die on the spot, and a young woman just happened to be there. It was unlikely, though, on that road lost in the middle of nowhere.

As my body crashed to the pavement, I felt my bones crack. I heard them too. An iron taste permeated my senses. I was paralyzed. My beautiful apparition approached me.

"Hold on, sir, I'll call for help!"

She was so pretty. But I could see the sadness in her eyes, the same sadness that overcame me a few years ago. I was so sorry for what I was about to do to her... Alas, I had no choice.

"My bag..."

Blood filled my mouth. It was slowly beginning to drown me. I coughed weakly to evacuate it, in little spurts.

"Forget your bag, sir, unless you've got a cell phone with you so I can call for help. I'm here! I'm here! Stay with me!"

"There..."

I pointed to my precious equipment with my eyes, I had no other way to do it. She grabbed it.

"You've got a phone!"

She took it with a nervous gesture.

"Take the purse... in my bag... It's for you..."

"We'll see about that later, if you don't mind. Hold on, I'll call for help."

"No... Take possession of my things, please... Save me from eternal damnation..."

She seemed totally lost, as if I'd said something incomprehensible. I must have, really. How could she understand? She'd just arrived in this world of darkness and couldn't have suspected its unalterable blackness.

Stunned, she finally put my bag on her lap and took the purse in her hands. I was saved! I let go, carried away in a whirlwind of nothingness.

24

Ember

The spell gnaws at my guts, unleashing a throbbing pain accompanied by strikes of lightning. Thousands of sharp blades plunge into my nonexistent flesh, forcing me to writhe in the vain hope of escaping this unbearable suffering. Helpless and unable to make the slightest move to help, I watch Believe, who remains immobile. On her swollen lip, a large cut lets her blood run down her chin before dropping to the ground. Her bruised cheekbone takes on strange colors as the hematoma settles.

Her white braid is now unraveled, little shaggy locks encircling her livid face and her silver eyes concealed by large, purplish circles. She's a shadow of the woman I met a few days ago, a pale counterfeit of the one I kissed. Humans are so fragile. She gives the impression of having already died, as if she has given up the game, exhausted by the frantic race of circumstances.

"Believ..."

Our assailants freeze.

"Did you hear that?" says one of them, trembling.

"He's here," confirms another, shivering.

If they can hear me, now's the time to speak up. It's my turn to dictate the rules!

"Let her go!"

Despite the pain spreading through every centimeter of my being, I feel a surge of power flowing back. My voice, which until now had mingled with the breath of the wind, thunders in a cavernous storm like a sinister warning.

"Don't!" shouts the man who seems to be leading the small assault group. "Carry out orders as quickly as possible!"

Although shaken by my presence—not to say terrified for some, whose knees knock together despite their steps—they comply. Two of them grab Believ's arms and drag her toward the exit.

Did I really believe they would obey me?

Ghosts are part of the landscape of this cursed abbey, as I understand it. That some are still impressed is astonishing, when you think about it.

My threats will have no echo in the face of these warriors, but I must carry them out. I must save Believ!

"Ember!" she screams.

As she begs me with a volume to tear her vocal cords, my heart rips out of my chest and crumbles to pieces. It can't end like this. She wanted to help me. I can't let her perish without intervening!

"Ember!"

Her voice fades, gradually blurred by the growing distance and wavering hopes.

"Get over here!"

"You didn't have to be so clever! You're going to tell us everything, otherwise..."

If not, they won't be content with torturing her. When they tire of mutilating her, they'll finish her off, like all those Sin Eaters sacrificed and exposed for the example she told me about.

She's going to die.

This revelation strikes me with an even sharper violence than the one that paralyzes me. Whatever the secrets of my demise, I cannot conceive of her dying in this way. I refuse to let her lose her life through my fault.

"Ember."

This time, her voice fades to a whisper.

She falls. Her small, frail body crashes to the ground with a dull thud before being shaken by impressive spasms.

"What's wrong with her?"

"Epilepsy?" worries one of the guards.

"It doesn't matter; just take her away!" interjects the chief, who clearly refuses to keep his share of humanity.

She's so pale, so disjointed, so...

The memory of our kisses comes back to me. The sweetness of her mouth, the taste of her tongue, the ardor of her body sparkling with desire. She brought me back to life, even if only for a few moments, when she seems determined to give up hers.

I don't want to!

"Believ! Liev! Liev! Lie. Li..."

My timbre reverberates under the dome, accompanied by a vengeful echo.

I tear myself away from the shackles of pain that lacerate me. My steps are heavy, painful, each one pulverizing my flesh, disintegrating me from the inside. How can I suffer so much when I no longer have a material body?

My body...

I see it. It's there, in front of me, asleep as when I met the woman who changed my death: serene and radiant.

At the cost of unbearable pain, I manage to reach the table on which it lies. My substance brushes against its toes without going through them. I've touched it!

"It's not letting up..."

Indeed, even though I can no longer see her, I can hear Believ's limbs banging frantically against the floor. What's happening to her? Why is this happening?

"We're wasting our time. Finish her off."

I, who naively believed that religious people were the bearers of peace, and who, not so long ago, was convinced that they protected honest people, now feel quite credulous. Although mankind denies it, the only thing they protect is their own personal interests, even if this is at the expense of their most innocent peers. Or their most devoted.

Now that she no longer serves their purposes, they're ready to eliminate her without the slightest consideration. Without a thought for those she'll leave behind. Without even a prayer for the salvation of her soul.

I grab my ankle and pull myself up onto the edge of the table. Feeling this inert body awakens strange sensations, a kind of primal instinct that spreads through my...

Veins!

I've reinvested my body! What a strange feeling. And yet, although the situation is hardly conducive to it, I'm thrilled to feel... alive again!

"Let her go!" I shout.

My voice is hoarse, my throat desperately dry, but no matter. The cavernous sound reverberates under the dome, and its echo makes the strongest of them tremble. I feel powerful, an unprecedented sensation, but a euphoric one. Although my body is heavy, it anticipates my thoughts. Before I know what to do, it's rushing toward the squadron whose weapons are pointed at Believ, who lies inert on the ground. Her agonizing tremors have ceased, but she hasn't regained consciousness. Her eyelids are closed, as mine were just a few minutes ago. Could she already be...?

No, no, no, no! I will *not* allow this to happen! We've come this far with the energy of despair, and yet here we are at the end of this quest. It can't end like this! As long as I'm alive—and that's putting it mildly—no one will harm Believ.

Carried along by the impulse of despair, I pounce on the guards, who remain frozen, so stunned that they're gripped by an intense terror. Am I that frightening?

"A capture spell! Hurry!"

I don't give them time. With Believ as my ultimate objective, I swoop down on the men and sweep them away with a single thought. I grab the lifeless body of my rescuer and hold it close to me. Despite her leather jacket, I can feel her heart beating timidly.

She's still alive. And I'll make sure she stays that way.

Suddenly, as the members of the divine squadron stir, there's a lightout. Like a blackout, in light. As a spectator of what's going on, I feel myself being sucked up by intense radiation, lifted into the air by the screams of the audience, divided between those fleeing to save their own miserable skins and those who claim that this will be their last chance to capture me.

A jet of flames bursts into the room, engulfing whatever it can. I tighten my grip on Believ, still unconscious.

Suddenly, just as I'm about to reach the ceiling, the vault collapses. A shower of rock and earth falls on us, burying our pursuers. Instinctively, I fall back and wrap myself around Believ, offering her my recovered body as a shield. If this collapse is going to kill anyone, I'm determined that it's going to be me. She will live.

When I come to, she's still there, but she doesn't seem to see me.

Nevertheless, I'm here, every moment of the day. It's as if we aren't evolving in the same dimension.

I'm relieved to see that she's taking over. She's doing a pretty good job of it too, scrupulously following the procedure I'd discovered in my notebook.

Yet here I am. Something hasn't gone according to plan. And if I haven't joined the Underworld, I'm not in Paradise either... Something's wrong, but I don't really know what.

***

Since then, I've been wandering alongside her, vainly trying to support and help her, hoping that one day she'll forgive me for dragging her into this mess.

Lately, she's been doing some really strange things. For some reason, she refused to perform a ceremony. She simply took the bread and threw the beer away, pocketing the six coins nonetheless.

I don't think that's a good idea. Alas, I don't know how to warn her, since she can't see or hear me!

If only she could keep quiet and stick to the rules, she'd have a tiny hope of saving her skin— and maybe her soul.

25

Believ

I open my eyes to a field of ruins bathed in an unearthly light. Orange rays sweep over the rubble surrounding me, enveloping me in a soft warmth.

Am I dead?

I find shelter below a wall, but the devastated landscape in front of me hasn't been so lucky.

I try to sit up straight and take in the strange, apocalyptic scenery. How did I end up in the middle of this rubble, from which emerge broken limbs at the ends of which probably lie the corpses of human beings?

There's nothing left of the subterranean tunnels, buried forever with their foul secrets. I scan my surroundings; only dust floats. No sign of a human presence; I remain alone. I begin to panic. Ember! Where is Ember? *Please, God, let him be alive somewhere, and not under my feet*. I try to suppress a sob.

My seizure must have been more violent than the previous ones; I have no memory of what happened. There's no time to lose. I must find my ghost without delay. Of course, I reason with myself that a spirit floats, that nothing tangible can reach it, but I do remember one thing: he was in a very bad way the last time I saw him and, despite all his huffing and puffing to come to my rescue, something prevented him from doing so.

I'm leaving the cave that seems to have protected me from a destructive collapse when, all of a sudden, the wall shifts! A frightful roar resounds behind my back! What the...?

Stunned, I turn around to face the improbable: a dragon! I can't help but recoil, although I'm not sure whether it's fear that's driving me or the need to understand what I'm seeing. What is this creature doing here? How come dragons exist?

No... The physical proof of what I've learned in the basement is staring me in the face. Magical creatures do exist, and I've been visited by the most extraordinary of them all.

Despite everything, an instinctive cry gets stuck in my throat.

Its mouth opens wide, revealing countless fangs that leave me no chance of survival. What relieves me is that I'm unlikely to suffer either.

"Believ. Is everything all right?"

That voice...

The mere vibration of that timbre moves me. Tears escape from my eyes, and I can't contain them. Is he really here?

"Don't be afraid, Believ. We did it. *You* did it..."

With my eyes locked on the azure eyes of the charcoal beast, whose warm breath comes through the imposing row of teeth, I struggle to gather my wits. What is he hinting at? Why does he remain hidden? Why is he leaving me at the mercy of this carnivorous creature?

"We did it?" I struggle to articulate.

"This is me. You gave me back my body and my identity. You saved me."

What does this mean?

"Y-you?" I stammer, flabbergasted, now recognizing the particular hue of those irises staring back at me.

"I'm Ember Crow. I'm a—"

"Dragon."

My voice is lost in the breeze. My stiff is a fucking dragon!

What does this mean?

Did I do the right thing by helping him? How could I have been on the right side by helping to eliminate him?

The questions keep coming, without ever finding a logical answer.

Magic exists, but dragons?

"Dragons exist, Believ."

"You're reading my mind again! Frankly, you're overdoing it!"

"Please forgive me."

This is the first time he's been so familiar. It's as if something has changed, as if the accomplishment of this mission has sealed the bond we established when our paths crossed. And yet, it's not a bright future that awaits us...

"What is it, my sweet?"

"My sweet?" Where did that come from again?

At the same time, I feel exhilarated by this new-found intimacy. I bite my tongue. Time is running out, and I'm not going to let myself be lulled by sweet words. I straighten up, trying to adopt a firmer posture.

"Nothing you can't handle. You're a dragon, and you've got your body back. Your life is back on track. As for mine..."

"Yours promises to be long and lovely. I'll help you find your son, I promise. I'll never leave you again."

Fine promises he'll never be able to keep. And for good reason: if his life is enjoying a revival, mine seems fatally compromised by my simple allegiance to the Sin Eaters.

"I don't understand," he laments. "Please explain."

Will he ever get out of my mind? He chuckles slightly, and it echoes strangely in my head.

"I'd never do that. I love you too much for that," he says, his tone now serious.

What did he just say?

My heart has just missed a beat. I freeze as I stare at him, magnificent and majestic. A dragon telling me he loves me is incongruous enough, but for it to be Ember, a ghost who's become a man again without really being one... It's just... No, in fact, I'm stunned, mainly because no one down here, apart from my son, has ever told me they love me. For a first-timer, I should be exploding with joy and euphoria. I should be jumping into his arms, doing or expressing something, but I'm still stunned.

That it comes from a chimerical being accentuates the exceptional nature of this moment. What am I saying? This whole adventure was extraordinary and pretty much doomed from the start. So, to add to this incredible story, the fact that three magical little words came from an equally magical being seems almost logical.

What about me? Who am I fooling besides myself? Because what I feel for him is genuine, and it's eating me up. I know the beginnings of a state of love; I've been in it enough to be able to identify the symptoms. And right now, as I stare at this heavenly creature, my heart swells with immense love and sorrow because there will be no happy ending for us. As I was pointing out, it was dead before it even started. What irony! What shitty timing too!

One day, I'm going to have to come to terms with this fate that's haunted me since birth. But I can't! Everything in me revolts at the thought of this tear that's about to begin. I need to scream my rage and distress. To cry out to heaven for a reason that's about to fall flat. The blatant injustice I've suffered for so many years finds an outlet in the outcome of our story. And there's nothing I can do about it. In this single moment, I hate Eltz, the whole Brotherhood, and the Church as a whole. If there really is a God in this universe and He's good, let Him help me, because I can't do it alone.

I pull myself together, clearing my throat, although a ball of distress clogs my windpipe. Damn! I feel like a part of me is going to be torn apart, and I'm going to suffer a thousand pains if I speak out loud. I contemplate the being for whom my heart has been beating for a few days—or has it always been? Time is playing tricks on me, and it's with a barely suppressed sob that I tell him my implacable truth.

"Ember, you don't understand. There is no 'us.' What we shared was an enchanted interlude in a sea of troubles, but I'm going to die," I exclaim, frustrated that I can't let myself dream because my situation is so shaky.

"One day, perhaps. And yet, nothing is less certain."

Although I can't make out his features, I can hear in his voice the certainty that he'll put his heart and soul into finding a way. I'm getting to know him. His conviction is the law. He's unwavering in his actions; he'll go through with it, whatever it takes. And it's this powerful personality that I've fallen in love with. Where I've simply followed a path laid down by others, he follows his own and never deviates from it.

I speak of him as a man, despite the aspects of his personality that I don't know. What do I know about magical creatures and their powers, other than what folklore has bequeathed us? But since they're all lies woven by the Church, I find it hard to put any faith in them. Speaking of faith, I haven't got a shred of it left.

"Not one day. Soon. Too soon," I assert, my voice firming.

There's no point in prolonging the suffering. I'll try to cope with mine, added to the lack of my child. I don't know how, but I'll find a way to survive. His, on the other hand, will destroy me. That's not a figure of speech. His pain will literally overwhelm me. I already felt it when we met. As long as it didn't leave him, it clung just as tightly to my heart. At this moment, I pray that the pain I'm about to inflict on him will be less intense than the loss of his identity and his body.

"Why?" he asks.

His tone suggests that he's genuinely taken aback by the lack of doubt in the wording of my reply. I owe him this vile and implacable truth, which I refrained from telling him earlier, not deeming it appropriate to reveal its content.

"Because if I stop feeding on sin, I'll be extinguished. No other nourishment can sustain me now. And you'll understand why I'm no longer interested in pursuing this profession, now that I know the whole mission was a sham! I've killed creatures! I've stripped them of their souls..."

Tears are now rolling down my cheeks, an expression of the terrible guilt that's choking me to death.

Even if I wasn't aware of it, I've condemned dozens of magical beings, maybe even hundreds. Who knows what the human element was in those I assisted? Were there any? Did I ever officiate for good?

"You..."

He falls silent, unable to complete his sentence, a devastating sadness drowning his steely gaze.

"These crises that control me are an expression of lack. Since we met, I haven't practiced my profession. I haven't fed myself. My addiction is consuming me little by little."

"You're exaggerating, aren't you?" he tries to reassure himself.

"I'm going to die, Ember."

My voice breaks, like our illusions crashing to the ground. I close my eyes to let my guilt and bottomless sorrow flow. A breath ruffles my hair. I raise my eyes instantly. He manages the feat of adopting a smaller size. The gigantic being is transformed into a dragon barely two meters tall.

With his wings, he embraces me and presses me against his muscular chest. I feel his heart beating behind the leather of his scaly skin, the heart that had been extinguished and whose executioner I almost was.

“I'm going to die...”

These last words make my destiny more palpable. I let myself be misled, carried away by the hope of finding Lewis. I lacked discernment and sacrificed myself to a cause that wasn’t my own, a cause I detest and will fight without mercy as long as I draw breath.

“I won't leave you, ever,” he murmurs in a hoarse breath that sounds like a promise of eternity. “Hang on, they're coming.”

Before I know what he's talking about, he's grabbing me with his powerful talons and carrying me away in the glow of the Welsh sunrise, the sun of legends.

And here I am, my hair blowing in the wind, admiring the landscape, clutching in my closed fist a small pebble slipped into my pocket earlier.

Over Dark Editions

Always follow your Dreams

overdarkeditions.com

Sienna Pratt

sienna_pratt_author

sienna_pratt_over_dark

over_dark_editions

sienna_pratt_over_dark

sienna_pratt_over_dark

Made in the USA
Monee, IL
31 October 2025

33412104R00132